Secrets...
& Lust

...Plus!

DO YOU **ACT** BEFORE YOU **THINK**?
TRY OUR FAB QUIZ AT
THE BACK OF THE BOOK

eyed Ellie with unconcealed curiosity as she approached the desk.

One of the two receptionists on duty looked up at her approach. 'May I help you?' she said.

'I'm Dr Renshaw,' said Ellie. 'Ellie Renshaw. I'm your new locum.'

'Oh, Dr Renshaw,' said the receptionist, 'we are expecting you. Pleased to meet you. I'm Jenny Smythe.' She turned to her colleague, a much younger woman. 'And this is Sophie Hall.'

'Hello, Jenny, Sophie.' Ellie smiled, aware that a ripple of interest had spread through the rows of waiting patients.

'I'll take you upstairs to our practice manager,' said Jenny, coming round the desk.

Ellie followed the receptionist upstairs where on the landing they were met by Andrea March, the practice manager whom Ellie had met previously at her interview with William Stafford, the senior partner.

'Ah, Dr Renshaw,' said Andrea, 'it's nice to see you again. Would you like to come straight along to your room?'

'Yes, please.' Ellie smiled and nodded at Jenny, who hurried back downstairs, no doubt to help Sophie cope with the inevitable Monday morning rush.

'You'll be using Judy Maxwell's room,' said Andrea. She led the way down a corridor then stopped in front of a door which she opened wide then stood back for Ellie to precede her into the room. 'This is the one,' she said. 'It's a nice, light, sunny room...' She paused then, turning to Ellie, she went on, 'You haven't met the other partners yet, have you?'

Ellie shook her head, 'No, only Dr Stafford, and I did briefly see Judy Maxwell.'

'They haven't started their surgeries yet,' Andrea replied. 'I would imagine they are all in their staff-room, having their early morning shot of caffeine. Would you like to come along and meet them now or would you rather wait until after surgery?'

'Well, I always say there's no time like the present,' said Ellie.

'OK, we'll go now. Leave your case here. We'll lock this door and I'll give you this set of keys—I'll explain what they are all for later,' said Andrea. 'I know Dr Stafford told you about the other partners,' she said as they began making their way further down the corridor. 'There's Reece Davies and Isobel Collingwood, and in the last few weeks a new partner has joined the team so you won't have heard about him. But don't worry, he's nice...very nice, in fact,' she added with a knowing little laugh.

Afterwards Ellie could have kicked herself for not asking the name of this new partner who was very nice, but at the time it didn't seem important—it would have been just another name to remember in a welter of names she was already struggling with. If only she had asked. It was a name that would have been instantly recognisable, a name she would have had no trouble remembering for it was burned on her memory for all time. But it would have made no difference anyway because there would have been absolutely nothing she could have done about it. She had signed a six-month contract with the Oakminster practice, while he was a full partner. But had she known, she would have been forewarned, would have had time, even if only moments, to prepare herself. As it was, Ellie was ushered into the doctors' staff-room—a large room lined with bookshelves. Several people rose to their feet from comfortable armchairs to greet her as Andrea announced her presence.

William Stafford was there, greeting her with a smile and a warm handshake. 'Dr Renshaw—Ellie,' he said in his cultured voice. 'Lovely to see you again.'

Reece Davies rose from his chair—a great bear of a man with a mane of dark hair and a full beard—his welcome every bit as warm as his partner's. Isobel Collingwood also greeted her then William Stafford spoke again. 'Ellie,' he said, 'we have a new partner.' She turned as he indicated a chair, which had been partly obscured by the open door, a chair from which the tall figure of a man rose.

Ellie's gaze met his and in that moment it was as if the world stood still. She found herself looking into a pair of eyes that were not quite green and not quite hazel, a pair of eyes which she would have known anywhere in the world. Her heart lurched painfully in her chest while her voice seemed to have deserted her completely.

'Hello, Ellie,' he said softly.

'Ellie,' said William, apparently oblivious to any tension, 'this is Luke.' He turned to the man. 'Luke, this is our locum, Ellie Renshaw…' He broke off as he realised that Luke had called Ellie by name before he'd introduced her. 'I say,' he said, looking from one to the other of them, 'do you two know each other?'

'Yes,' said Luke, the pause that followed so fleeting that probably only Ellie herself was aware of it. 'We used to work together, didn't we, Ellie?'

It was a good job he'd answered, thought Ellie, because she was still having difficulty finding her voice after the shock of seeing him again. But even as she struggled to find her voice the significance of his words struck her. Was that all she had been to him—someone he had once worked with?

Then she heard someone speak. 'Yes,' they said, the voice cool, light, 'we did, but it was a long time ago—I don't remember exactly when.' And she realised the voice was her own and that from somewhere deep inside she had drawn up the resources to deliver a fitting reply.

'It was four years ago,' he said, his eyes never leaving her face as he took her hand. There was a second shock as his skin touched hers and she felt herself being transported back to hot summer nights under starry skies and cold winter days before blazing log fires as memories crowded her mind and threatened to throw her completely off balance. 'And it was at St Batholomew's—a hospital in the Midlands,' he added, presumably for the benefit of the others. 'A and E, to be precise.'

'Well, well,' said William, 'what a small world it is. But nice for you, Ellie—I always think it's an advantage to find a familiar face in a new environment.'

'Yes, quite,' she replied tersely, and any irony in her tone seemed lost on the senior partner. More polite small talk followed but Ellie found it incredibly difficult to concentrate on what was being said and longed to get back to the seclusion of her consulting room so that she could recover from the shock. All she could think about while she was in this staffroom was the fact that Luke Barron was standing only a few feet away from her and hadn't actually taken his eyes off her.

'So, are you happy with that, Ellie?' To her horror Ellie realised that William had been talking to her and she hadn't heard a word he'd been saying. Furthermore, he'd actually posed a question and was now waiting for her reply.

'I'm sorry...' she began, and to her further embarrassment it was Luke who came to her rescue, Luke, who was the only person there who may have had an insight into how she was feeling.

'I'm sure Ellie is only too happy to take over Judy Maxwell's patient list,' he said smoothly. 'Isn't that so, Ellie?'

'Oh, yes,' she said. 'Yes, of course.'

'Well, that's a relief, I can tell you,' said Reece. 'We've had locums in the past who are only prepared to take the extra surgeries and temporary residents— it makes life so much easier if we don't have to split the absent partner's list between us.'

'I consider that's why I'm here,' said Ellie.

'I can see we're going to get along just fine.' Reece gave a beaming smile.

'Come back to your room, Ellie,' said Andrea, 'and I'll show you the computer system and a few other essentials you need to know in order to take surgeries. You'll be pleased to know we haven't put you down for one this morning so that you have a little time to familiarise yourself with the place.'

Still aware of Luke's eyes on her, with an overwhelming sense of relief Ellie left the room.

'You didn't know Luke Barron was here, did you?' asked Andrea curiously as they walked back along the corridor.

'No,' Ellie agreed faintly, 'I didn't.'

'Know him well, did you?' Clearly Andrea had picked up something, either her shock on seeing Luke or the unmistakable tension between them.

'Er…yes, you could say that.' Ellie hesitated, wondering just how much she should say bearing in mind she hardly knew this woman and had no idea how far she could trust her integrity. 'Trouble is…we didn't part on particularly good terms.'

'Ah, well, like you say, it was a long time ago,' said Andrea sympathetically. 'Maybe you'll find he's changed.'

'Maybe,' Ellie agreed, but deep inside she knew he hadn't. Luke Barron was Luke Barron, and she didn't imagine for a moment he would have changed one little bit. Why, she thought after Andrea had left her alone to familiarise herself with her room, he even looked the same. The dark blond hair cut the same, the lean but solid frame without an ounce of spare flesh, the finely chiselled features and strong jaw, and those eyes—tawny, she'd once heard someone describe them, like something you might expect to find in the jungle. She shivered slightly as she recalled the way he had looked at her, reawakening memories of how things had once been between them, the way that things could never be again.

As she'd said to Andrea, she'd had no idea that Luke was in partnership at the Oakminster practice. The last she had heard was that he was still working on an exchange contract in the States. If she had known he was there, she doubted she would have taken on the appointment.

She sat in front of the computer, staring at the screen with unseeing eyes and wondering what she could do about the situation she now found herself in. The sense of shock at seeing Luke again was slowly beginning to ebb away, leaving her with a feeling almost of desperation as it sank in that she was going to be expected to work alongside him and have daily contact with him for the next six months. It was the last thing she wanted, but she really didn't see there was any way she could get round it. She had signed a contract with the practice that was legally binding and she couldn't see that merely not wanting to work with someone constituted a legitimate reason for terminating that contract.

'Did you know I was here, Ellie?' She swung round sharply from the computer to find Luke standing in the open doorway. She'd been so lost in her thoughts that she hadn't even heard him open the door. 'I did knock,' he added, catching sight of her expression, 'but I don't think you heard me.'

She felt a line of sweat trickle down her neck then on, further, between her shoulder blades. 'No,' she said, 'I didn't hear you.' She took a deep breath. 'Neither did I know you worked here, Luke.' She paused. 'Did you know it was me who was coming as locum?' It was almost a demand and she saw him flinch slightly at her tone.

'Not until last week,' he said. 'I knew Judy Maxwell was going off on maternity leave and I knew that cover had been found for her, but I didn't know the name of the locum.'

'Until last week.'

'Yes,' he agreed. 'Last week I happened to see a letter concerning your appointment and when I saw the name Eloise Renshaw I thought it highly likely it would be you.'

'And what did you think?'

'I thought how nice it would be to see you again after all this time,' he said. A certain look came into his eyes, a look that Ellie remembered only too well, and she looked quickly away. 'And it is nice, isn't it, Ellie? Don't you agree?' he added, lowering his head slightly in an attempt to look into her eyes again.

'In spite of the circumstances in which we parted?' she asked coolly, still avoiding his gaze.

'A tiff,' he said, 'no more than that. We'd already agreed to part at that point if my memory serves me rightly.'

'Yes,' she agreed in the same cool tone. 'We had. As you were going off to the States, there didn't seem to be a lot of point in keeping things going. If my memory serves me correctly, you didn't waste too much time replacing me.'

'Replacing you?' He stared at her.

'At the leaving party?'

'Oh, that.' He dismissed it with a gesture. 'It was nothing. I'd drunk far too much and Susie or whatever her name was just happened to be there.'

'You don't have to justify it to me.' She shrugged. 'Like you say, by then we had parted anyway.' There was silence for a moment then she said, 'So what happened to the States—did you get fed up with that as well?'

He frowned. 'No, of course not. My contract ended there and I decided to come home.'

'So why here, why Oakminster?' There was a note of desperation in her voice.

He shrugged. 'Why not? I know the area and when I saw the advertisement for a partner in the practice, I thought it seemed like a good idea. But...' He paused and stared intently at her again. 'What about you?'

'What do you mean?' Her voice was sharper than

she had intended as her brain raced ahead, trying to anticipate what questions he would ask her.

'Well, I was surprised to find you doing locum work…'

'What you mean is you thought I would have secured a partnership by now—is that it?' She tried her best to keep her voice steady, her tone casual but fearing that she was failing miserably and that he would instantly see through the façade.

'Well, yes,' he admitted, 'I suppose that is exactly what I mean. You were so ambitious, Ellie, you always knew exactly the way you wanted your career to go.'

'Did I?' She shrugged again, nonchalantly, she hoped. 'Well, I guess things change. Locum work suits me at the moment.'

'You only work part time?' He was sounding curious again.

'Yes. And before you ask,' she said, leaping in and hoping to deflect any further awkward questions, 'I'm also living with my mother. We—she—had some problems and this arrangement that we have now works just fine for us both.'

'I see,' he said slowly. 'Well…like I said before, it is good to see you again, Ellie, and I hope that anything that may or may not have happened between us in the past will not jeopardise the way we get on here.'

'Of course not,' she said crisply. 'After all, we are both professionals.'

'Quite,' he replied. 'And that is the reason why I led the others to believe that we had been merely colleagues in the past—I thought that would save any embarrassment.' That look was back in those tawny eyes, the look that could throw professionalism to the winds.

'I agree,' she said quickly, 'absolutely. There is no need whatever for them to know anything else—it's in the past and totally irrelevant now.'

For a fleeting moment she thought she detected some other emotion in his eyes, almost regret, but she couldn't be sure. Whether that regret was because they had parted or because they were now dismissing what had happened between them as having little consequence, she was even less sure.

'I'll leave you to get on now.' He spoke almost briskly. 'If there's anything you want or need, I'm just down the corridor.' He paused. 'We'll have to get together some time and have a chat over old times,' he said.

'I must get on and sort a few things out,' she said, waving her hand towards the desk, neither agreeing nor disagreeing with him.

'OK.' He held up his hands, the gesture almost defensive, and then he was gone. Ellie sank back into her chair, thankful that she hadn't been standing because she doubted that her knees would have taken her weight.

It was too cruel, him turning up like this again, she thought as she gazed helplessly at the computer screen. She really hadn't thought she would ever see him again, although at the back of her mind she had, of course, always known there was a possibility that she might. She had hoped he might stay in the States because at one time that had been all he had seemed to want to do, all he'd been able to talk about, in fact. That had been one of the reasons why she had tried to keep some sort of distance between them. Knowing that she couldn't allow herself to become too involved with him, only to have him move on and go abroad to work. But it had all been pretence. Of course it had, because she had become involved with him, had adored him, in fact, which had made it all the more impossible when the time had come to part. He, too, had been wary of commitment as he had steadily built his career and had seemed only too willing to end their relationship as his impending departure had drawn close.

They had argued, too, right at the very end over that farewell night at the hospital social club and the young nurse who had accompanied him, clinging to him like a limpet. They'd parted in anger after an ugly scene outside the club, and after that he'd left for the States and she hadn't seen him again—until now.

She shifted in her chair. How did she feel on seeing him again? It had been a shock, there was no denying that. If she was really honest, her emotions had been turned upside down. Was there more or was that where it ended? She stood up and stretched, looking out the window at the busy market scene in the street below. She would have liked to think that was all it was: a chance meeting between two old friends— well, lovers really. But while she might just be able to get away with that to others—the staff, for example, or even her mother, although she feared that might be a bit more difficult—she knew it was no earthly use lying to herself.

She had been hopelessly in love with Luke Barron in the past, even though she doubted he'd felt the same way about her. All that seeing him today had done had been to rekindle those feelings. But while she might easily hide those feelings from others, she knew the one thing she must guard against at all costs was revealing them to Luke, because this time there was far too much at stake. She would carry out her duties at the practice to the very best of her ability because she had no other option where the terms of her contract were concerned. She would be polite and friendly towards Luke in their everyday dealings, and she would guard against any contact with him outside the practice.

With those resolutions finally and firmly in place, she turned back to her desk and the many tasks she needed to do to get herself ready to take her place as the Oakminster practice's new locum.

CHAPTER TWO

IT HAD been easier for him—that first meeting. Luke accepted that because he had known he was about to see her again, but for Ellie it had been a shock—a tremendous shock if the look in her eyes had been anything to go by. His own heart had been hammering in his chest as he had waited for Andrea to bring her up to the staffroom, and when she had turned towards him and seen that he was the new partner he had felt his mouth go dry.

This was what he had hoped for, the chance to see Ellie again, ever since he had seen the advertisement for a partner for the Oakminster practice. This was the area where Ellie's family had always lived and he'd thought there might be a chance of seeing her again, although he'd had to accept the fact that the chance was pretty remote. A lot could have happened in four years. She could have moved away herself—to another part of the country or even abroad, as he had done—or she could quite easily be married, although he found himself hoping desperately that wasn't the case. He only had himself to blame if she was, he told himself ruefully. He'd had his chance with Ellie and really, if he was honest, he'd blown it because in those days he quite simply hadn't been ready to settle down. His career had been the most important thing and that crucial move to the States which, in all fairness, had been arranged even before he and Ellie had met.

And Ellie herself hadn't seemed too ready for any sort of commitment—in fact, it had been she who had suggested they call it a day just before he'd gone abroad. He'd agreed because he'd thought that had been what she'd wanted. Then, of course, had come that ridiculous, drunken episode at the club when he'd become entangled—literally—with a girl from Orthopaedics. Ellie had seen him making a spectacle of himself and bitter words had followed. He'd left for the States shortly after that without seeing Ellie again.

While at the time he had felt indignant—it had been Ellie who had suggested they end their relationship, so what right had she to make a fuss about what he did afterwards?—since then he had found himself missing her and wishing they hadn't been so hasty. He'd tried writing once to the hospital where they had both worked, hoping they would forward his letter to Ellie if she'd moved on, but he had received no reply and he'd gradually accepted the fact that she really didn't want any further contact with him.

But he couldn't forget her. Somehow she was always there at the edges of his mind, and if he closed his eyes he could picture her as she had been in that magical summer they had shared—the woodland walks they'd taken together, with the sunlight filtering through the trees onto her pale blonde hair so that it shone like spun silk, the way she would laugh at something he'd said, tossing her head so that the breeze would catch tendrils of her hair, whipping them across her face, or the way she would reach up and gently touch his face with the tips of her fingers as they made love.

There had been others since he had been away—

of course there had. Four years was a long time, but for some reason there had not been anyone who had reached him quite like Ellie had done.

And now that they had met again he wasn't even too sure that she had been particularly pleased to see him. Shocked, yes, but pleased? He really didn't know. He had gained the impression from the short talk they'd had when he'd gone to her room that she had been quite relieved at his suggestion that they shouldn't broadcast the fact that they'd been more than colleagues in the past. Maybe she was embarrassed or—perish the thought—ashamed of her association with him.

This wasn't quite how he'd planned things. He'd fondly imagined that if he did find her again she would have been as pleased to see him as he was to see her, but somehow it hadn't quite seemed to work out that way. Oh, he'd been pleased to see her—in fact, he'd hardly been able to contain himself when he'd been waiting for her to come into the staffroom.

But when she'd seen him—apart from being shocked, which he had expected—there had been something else, some other reaction, and he wasn't entirely sure what it had been. If there had been pleasure at seeing him again it had only been momentary—a fleeting thing that had been gone in the blink of an eye, so fast that he wondered now if he hadn't imagined it. There had been something else as well, something elusive, and it was that element that bothered him because he couldn't quite define it. Surely it hadn't been horror at realising that he was there in the very practice where she was to work? Surely he wasn't that bad? And what they'd once shared, had it been so terrible?

Of course it hadn't, he told himself firmly. It had been good, wonderful, and he was pretty certain that she had felt the same way. At least, at the time he'd thought she'd felt that way—so what could have changed since? Surely the reason couldn't solely be that crazy argument that had broken out in the hospital car park that night when he had been with Susie. Maybe it wasn't that, but there was definitely something that had changed.

There was always the chance that she was married, of course, and if that were so, he would simply have to accept it. She hadn't been wearing a wedding ring, but that didn't necessarily mean anything. Some people, he knew, didn't wear any jewellery, especially if they were handling any sort of chemicals.

He was still puzzling over Ellie's reaction at seeing him when his first patient of the morning arrived.

Local businessman Ritchie Austin was in his forties and had recently been complaining of chest pains.

'Your blood pressure is raised again, Ritchie,' said Luke as he checked the reading, 'so I want to do a twenty-four-hour monitor so we can get a clearer picture.'

'What does that mean?' Ritchie looked alarmed.

'It's a very simple procedure,' Luke explained. 'We strap a monitor to your arm and it takes readings every hour through the day and every two hours through the night.'

'And what if it's high all the time?'

'Then we put you on some medication to lower the pressure and we also talk about some lifestyle changes.'

'What do you mean, lifestyle changes?' Ritchie

looked even more alarmed. 'I don't like the sound of that. I like my life just the way it is.'

'Maybe, but it could be threatened if some changes aren't made now.'

'What sort of changes?' Ritchie scowled.

'Well, for a start, you need to stop smoking.'

'How did I know you were going to say that?' he said gloomily.

'I mean it, Ritchie,' said Luke. 'Also, you need to cut down on the alcohol. We also need to look at your diet. I suspect there's rather too much salt and fat intake.'

'Life won't be worth living at this rate,' muttered Ritchie. 'I suppose you're going to say I have to cut out sex next.'

'Actually, no. Sex is a form of exercise that is good. But speaking of exercise, do you do any sport?'

'Not really.' Ritchie shook his head. 'Don't have the time—too busy working. I occasionally knock a few balls around the golf course, but that's only usually when I've got some business contacts to make.'

'You do need to do some form of regular exercise,' said Luke.

'Apart from sex, you mean?' Ritchie grinned.

'Yes, apart from sex. It needn't be anything too strenuous—brisk walking a few times a week will help. I guess you take the car everywhere.'

'Too right I do. I haven't worked all this time to get my top-of-the-range Jag, only to leave it in the garage.'

Even Luke laughed at that. Growing serious again, he said, 'I mean it, Ritchie—a few fundamental changes now could put years on your life.'

'Well, I suppose we all have to die of something,' said Ritchie with a shrug.

'True,' Luke agreed, 'but have you ever stopped to think about the nature of that death?'

'What do you mean?' Ritchie narrowed his eyes.

'Well, what you are building up for yourself by smoking, overeating and taking no exercise could result in a sudden, premature death. On the other hand, it could give you ten to twenty years of appalling ill health before you die—years during which your life would become a complete and utter misery. It's worth thinking about. Now, in the meantime, in view of your recent chest pains, I'm going to refer you to a cardiologist.'

That seemed to have more impact on Ritchie than anything else that had been discussed, and he finally left the surgery more subdued than when he had come in. Luke sighed as he entered Ritchie's details onto the computer, together with the referral request. Trying to persuade patients to change their lifestyles and alter the habits of a lifetime was one of the most difficult challenges that he and his fellow GPs had to face.

Throughout that busy morning surgery Luke's thoughts frequently turned to Ellie. She had seemed to want to be left alone to come to grips with the workings of the practice in her own time, but by the end of the morning Luke could stand it no longer and on a sudden impulse decided to ask her to have lunch with him. He was certain she would benefit from a run-down of the practice—the staff and the patients—and if she still didn't want that, maybe they could talk of old times. Perhaps that was just what was needed to clear the air between them, he told himself as he strode along the corridor to her room.

But in the event, that was as far as his intentions went for her room was empty, and when he enquired from Andrea where Ellie was, it was to be told that she'd gone home.

'Already?' He stared at Andrea. 'Was there anything wrong?'

'No, I don't think so.' Andrea shook her head. 'But she's only doing part time. Had you forgotten?'

'Actually, yes, I had,' he said.

'She will be starting Judy's surgeries tomorrow morning.'

'Right.' He was disappointed at not seeing her, but there was nothing he could do about it. He would simply have to wait until the next day.

Home for Ellie and Jamie was in an old, whitewashed, thatched cottage on the edge of the village. It was where Ellie had grown up with her mother Barbara and her father Peter. Her father had been the local GP and her mother had worked as an illustrator for a London publisher. Life had been happy and secure, but when Ellie had been seventeen her father had been killed in a plane crash after attending a medical conference in Singapore. It had been a dreadful time for his widow and daughter as they'd faced an uncertain future without him, but the medical insurance from the crash, together with Peter's pension fund, had enabled Barbara and Ellie to remain in the cottage. Eventually Ellie had gone away to medical school and Barbara had resumed working from home as a freelance illustrator of children's books.

Now, as Ellie parked her car at the side of the cottage and walked around to the back, she found her mother seated at her drawing board in the small studio that had once been an outhouse.

'Hi, Mum.' Ellie raised one hand in greeting.

'Hello, darling.' Barbara looked up and smiled. 'How did it go?'

'Oh, not too bad, I suppose.' Ellie pulled a face. 'It'll take me a while to get into it. Did Jamie go into nursery OK?'

'Yes, he was fine.' Barbara glanced at the clock on the wall. 'There's a good hour before you need to pick him up—time for a cup of tea and a sandwich.'

'I'll put the kettle on,' said Ellie, and walked into the large kitchen.

'It's still hot,' said Barbara, as she followed her. 'The weatherman said it wouldn't break for at least another three days or so.'

'It's too hot to work.' Ellie lifted the teapot down from its shelf.

'So what's your consulting room like?' asked Barbara as she took mugs and plates from a cupboard.

'Nice. Quite pleasant really.'

'And the rest of the staff?'

'Ah, well,' said Ellie darkly, 'that's another story.'

Barbara looked over her shoulder. 'Oh?' she said. 'Was there a problem?'

'You could say that.' Ellie nodded then to her horror noticed that her hands were shaking. 'Actually, Mum,' she said, rapidly coming to a decision, 'I've had rather a shock.'

'Oh, darling, whatever is it?' Barbara stared at her then must have realised how distressed she was for she said, 'Look, we'll take our lunch outside and sit in the shade and you can tell me all about it.'

Ten minutes later they were seated under the apple trees at the white garden table and Barbara had poured the tea and was obviously waiting for Ellie to enlighten her.

'There was a new partner,' said Ellie as she struggled to find the right words, 'one I hadn't known about, who hadn't been there or even been mentioned at the interview.'

'So who was it?' Barbara stared at her daughter then must have seen something in her eyes. 'You're not telling me it was Luke,' she said quietly at last.

Ellie nodded. 'Yes, that's exactly who it was.'

'Oh, Ellie.' The dismay in Barbara's voice was obvious.

'Yes.'

'I always feared this would happen,' said Barbara at last, shaking her head. 'I always said that one day—'

'I know, Mum. I know that's what you said.' Ellie held up one hand, the gesture somehow defensive but at the same time making her appear vulnerable. 'But I really didn't think he would come back.' She drew in her breath. 'It was a terrific shock, I can tell you,' she added helplessly.

'I'm sure it was,' said Barbara sympathetically. 'So what is he doing here? You thought he was still in America, didn't you?'

'Yes, I did.' Ellie sighed. 'It seems he missed England. Anyway, he's returned and he's firmly ensconced at Oakminster.'

'Presumably he was just as shocked to see you,' said Barbara quickly.

'Not as much as I was to see him,' said Ellie wryly. 'He, apparently, had seen a letter concerning my appointment as locum so he had been forewarned. I nearly collapsed when I saw him in the staffroom.'

'So what are you going to do?' asked Barbara after a moment.

'What can I do?' Ellie shrugged. 'I've signed a contract—it would be an expensive business to get out of it. I guess I shall just have to grit my teeth and get on with it. At least it's only for six months. Mind you, it promises to be the longest six months of my life.'

There was a long silence between them as they continued to eat the sandwiches and drink their tea, a silence during which the only sounds to be heard were the buzzing of a bee as it hovered over the honeysuckle that sprawled over the trellis fence and the distant sound of traffic on the dual carriageway that bypassed the village.

'I wasn't actually meaning that,' said Barbara at last, breaking the silence. 'What I meant was, what are you going to do about…?'

'I know what you meant, Mum,' said Ellie, interrupting her, 'and the answer is nothing.'

Barbara was silent again then, leaning forward, she said, 'Ellie, I think you need to think very carefully about this.'

'There's nothing to think about,' said Ellie with a shrug. 'I made my decision a long time ago and I see no reason to change it now.'

'I understand why you made that decision,' said Barbara slowly, 'although I didn't necessarily agree with it, but to all intents and purposes Luke had supposedly gone right out of your life.' She paused. 'The circumstances have changed now,' she went on after a moment.

'I don't see it should make any difference,' said Ellie stubbornly.

'But he's back, he's here, on your very doorstep…' Barbara protested.

'I still see no reason for anything to change.'

'So you don't intend telling him about Jamie?' Barbara stared at her.

'No.' Ellie shook her head. 'Why should I?'

'Well, for a start, don't you think there's a very good chance that he will find out you have a three-year-old son?'

'He may do.' Ellie shrugged again. 'Although I don't intend allowing my job to intrude into my private life.'

'You may find that more difficult than you think. You know what it's like, how social events creep in— celebrations, someone leaves and they have a party— that sort of thing. And besides, didn't you tell them at your interview that you have a child—that that was the reason you wanted part-time work?'

'I may have mentioned it to William Stafford—I don't know, I can't remember.' The stubborn look was still on Ellie's features. 'But even if I did, even if they do know I have a child, they don't know his age. And, besides, it doesn't prove anything. Even if Luke does find out,' she went on and there was a slight note of hysteria in her voice now, 'it still won't prove a thing. I could have had a relationship after he left…'

'I still think you should have told him at the time,' said Barbara. With a sigh she stood up and picked up the teatray then stood for a moment looking down at her daughter. 'He had a right to know, Ellie—and I still think he has a right to know, just as Jamie has a right to know.' Turning away, Barbara walked back to the cottage, leaving Ellie still sitting beneath the apple trees, her thoughts in turmoil.

It had been a shock when she had discovered she was pregnant, mainly because it couldn't have come at a worse time, and partly because she and Luke had been so careful during their relationship. There had been one time she recalled that they had been careless and unbelievably, if inevitably, that had been when she had conceived. Her discovery had come after she and Luke had decided to end their relationship in order to pursue their careers. Ellie had already worked out that Luke hadn't really wanted any further commitment, that he hadn't yet been ready to settle down, and rather than allow herself to become even more involved with him, which she feared would lead to even greater heartbreak in the long run, she had reluctantly allowed him to believe that she too had been wary of further commitment. Their parting had been imminent anyway as he'd prepared to leave for his new job in the States, and Ellie had reached the stage where she had just wished he would go so that she could attempt to get on with her life and try to put him out of her mind. It had been then that she'd missed a period and an early test had confirmed her pregnancy. She had agonised for a whole week over what she should do. She could have had a termination and no one would have been any the wiser, she could have had the baby and brought it up alone or she could have told Luke and they could have decided together.

After a great deal of heart-searching she almost decided to tell Luke—but then there came that night at the social club when he made such a spectacle of himself. He lost no time in replacing her with Susie Farrell, and she changed her mind. Luke eventually left for America totally oblivious to the fact that he had fathered a child, and Ellie was forced to face reality alone.

In the end she confided in her mother but by then she had decided that for her termination was not an option and that she would go ahead and have the baby and bring it up alone. Her mother, as Ellie had known she would, stood by her from the very start, although she voiced her opinions where Luke was concerned.

'You should tell him,' she said.

'No.' Ellie was adamant. 'I don't want him to know.'

'But why?' Barbara was nothing if not persistent.

'We have already decided to end our relationship— it is over. Luke made it quite plain that his career comes first, that he doesn't want commitment, and the last thing he wants to do is settle down. Can you see a baby fitting into that agenda?'

'Maybe not,' Barbara reluctantly agreed, 'but I still think he should be given the chance to decide for himself.'

Ellie didn't tell her mother that she had almost decided to tell Luke before that last bitter scene between them, of how hurt she had been, but instead all she said was, 'It would never work.'

'It might.' Barbara stuck to her guns. 'It might be the very thing he needs to make him settle down.'

'Come back because of the baby, you mean?' Ellie shuddered. 'No, thanks. If he didn't want to settle down with me in the first place, there's no way I want him thinking I'm using this baby to trap him. Just leave it, Mum, please, because this is the way it's going to be.'

And that was indeed the way it was. In all fairness, her mother didn't refer to Luke again but gave Ellie all the help she needed, first as her pregnancy progressed and later, after Ellie moved back to live at the cottage, and when Jamie was born, it was Barbara who was at her side.

It was fortunately a relatively easy pregnancy but the labour was long, leaving Ellie exhausted after giving birth to a healthy nine-pound son. But it was all worth it for as she held her son and he stared intently at her with a deep blue stare she lost her heart for the second time in her life.

'He's beautiful,' whispered Barbara as she gazed at her grandson.

'Who does he look like?' asked the midwife.

'Oh, I think he has a look of my late husband, Ellie's father,' said Barbara firmly. 'Don't you think so, Ellie?'

'Yes,' Ellie agreed weakly, knowing full well that the baby in her arms looked exactly like his own father.

Somehow, in the weeks and months that followed, they managed as Ellie began to pick up the pieces of her life. Barbara continued to work at her illustrations from home and eventually, when Jamie was eight months old, Ellie registered him in a local nursery and returned to part-time locum work.

And really, she thought as a welcome breeze stirred the branches of the apple tree above her, everything had been fine—until now, until Luke had come back into their lives. And now, if she was really honest, everything was far from fine because the whole fabric of the happy existence that she had built up here at the cottage with her mother and Jamie was suddenly under threat.

CHAPTER THREE

ELLIE went to pick Jamie up from his nursery school and as the little boy ran to meet her she felt a pang deep inside as she realised just how much like Luke he was. That deep baby blue of his eyes had changed and, while they were not quite the same tawny colour of his father's, they were certainly no longer blue. Likewise, his hair, dark at birth, had changed to blond. Quite apart from the little boy's colouring, it was his features and his expressions that so closely mirrored his father's, and it was that which caused her heart now to miss a beat. While she had always been vaguely aware of these things, it had taken the reappearance of Luke in her life to throw them sharply into focus.

'Hello, darling.' She crouched down beside the little boy as he proudly presented her with the painting he had done that day and a cardboard cut-out figure of a dinosaur. 'These are beautiful,' she said, duly examining his work. 'Are they for me?'

He nodded solemnly, then caught sight of the football she carried in a plastic string bag. 'Football!' he said with glee.

'Yes.' Ellie nodded. Taking his hand, she said goodbye to the nursery assistant then led him outside. She knew Jamie loved to kick his football with her, and because there was no room for such games in the cottage garden she often took him to the village green. But somehow today was different. As they kicked the

34

ball to one another and Jamie shrieked with delight, Ellie was acutely aware that this was the sort of pursuit that little boys enjoyed with their fathers. Even in most of the one-parent families she knew, fathers more often than not appeared at weekends and took their children out.

Had she been wrong in her decision? she wondered as she watched Jamie run and pick up the ball and run back to her. She had never doubted what she had done before because she'd had no reason to. Luke had gone right out of her life long before Jamie's birth and she'd had no reason to believe that he would ever come back. But he was back now. Was it her duty to tell him, was it her duty to unite father and son? Her mother seemed to think it was, but Ellie was well aware that a lot of her mother's views on such things were old-fashioned, and quite often had no bearing on life in today's world, but rather on some idealised version of how she would like life to be.

As Jamie kicked the ball again, Ellie tried to imagine what it would be like if she were to tell Luke. Where on earth would she start? It was hardly something that could be casually tossed into conversation over morning coffee in the staffroom. *Oh, by the way, after you'd gone to the States, I had your baby. I decided not to tell you about it, but now that you've come back I thought perhaps you'd like to know.* She shuddered at the very thought. The telling would be bad enough, but what of the reaction? How on earth would Luke take such a bombshell? Would he tell her she had been foolish for allowing the pregnancy to continue? Would he be angry with her for not telling him he had a child? Maybe he would deny all responsibility and wash his hands of the whole business, and that particular reaction would probably be the hardest to bear.

Surely, in spite of what her mother said, it would be far better if Luke never knew? That way there would be no anger or recriminations, no rejection or denial. With a sigh she sat down in the shade of an oak tree on one of the wooden benches that surrounded the village green while Jamie abandoned his football and became far more interested in a cluster of woodlice around the base of the tree.

No, it would be far better if Luke knew nothing. For the next six months she mustn't become tempted at any time to tell him what had happened. She felt fairly confident that she could manage that. It would mean she would have to have as little contact with him as possible outside working hours, but she didn't imagine that would pose too much of a problem.

What she would have to safeguard against, of course, was him finding out in some other way. He would probably find out that she was a single parent. What she would have to prevent was him actually seeing Jamie and working out his age or even recognising the resemblance to himself. Did people do that—see themselves in a child? Or was it only something that other people saw and pointed out to them? Whatever the case, it would be far safer if he didn't see Jamie. And, really, the likelihood of him doing so was pretty remote. Most of Jamie's time was spent at the cottage or at his nursery school—apart, of course, from times like this when she took him out. Ellie found herself glancing apprehensively over her shoulder. There was nothing, of course, to prevent Luke driving past, even now. At that very moment he could drive by, see her, stop the car and come over. He would then automatically ask about Jamie.

What would she do then? Would she pretend he was from another relationship? She really didn't know. If she did, would he believe her? And if he didn't, what then? What if he wanted rights to his son? She stood up abruptly. 'Jamie,' she said, 'come on, it's time to go.'

'Don't want to go,' he said, without looking up from the woodlice.

'Yes, come on,' she said. 'It's teatime. Let's go and find Grandma.'

Reluctantly, with one last wistful look at the woodlice family, Jamie trailed after Ellie as they made their way across the green towards the cottage.

Home, for Luke, since his arrival in Oakminster, had been an apartment above the auction rooms in the oldest part of the town. Fortunately it had its own entrance so he was spared from having to fight his way through hordes of enthusiastic bargain hunters every time he went in or out of the premises. It was a large, airy apartment with two good-sized bedrooms and living space, most of which was lined with what seemed like acres of wooden panelling painted a soft dove grey. It reminded Luke of the house he'd stayed in while he'd been in New England. He hoped to move on in time, maybe buy his own property, but for the time being the apartment served his purpose.

That first night after Ellie had joined the practice he was restless, prowling the apartment and not really knowing whether he wanted to go out or to stay in. It had shaken him, seeing Ellie again, just as he had suspected it might. But it had been her reaction at seeing him that had haunted him ever since. He still couldn't quite pinpoint the exact nature of that reaction. Had she been pleased to see him again or not? In the end he stayed at home, sending out for a take-away and attempting to deal with some paperwork—but failing miserably because images of Ellie kept coming into his mind.

He slept badly, but by the morning he had made up his mind that the only way he could put paid to all his speculation was for him to ask her. If she had been pleased to see him, fine, they could take it from there. If she hadn't, the thing was to find out why and try to deal with the problem. He could hardly believe that she was still upset by the way they had parted, but if it was that, he would simply have to work at putting things right. Maybe she would agree to starting afresh, like they had just met for the first time, like there was no history between them. And if that meant him wooing her all over again then so be it. His heart thumped almost painfully at the very thought. Wooing Ellie had been pretty amazing the first time around—the second time might be even better.

It was with these upbeat thoughts in his mind that Luke arrived for work and just for one crazy moment, as he drove into the staff car park and saw Ellie getting out of her car, he thought perhaps his moment had come much earlier than he would have dreamed possible. He switched off his car engine and almost flung himself out of the car, but as he did so a second car drew in alongside his and he was forced to stand back and wait.

By the time that Reece had stepped out of his car Ellie had crossed the car park and was heading for the main entrance and Luke was forced to watch help-lessly as she disappeared into the building.

'She's a cracker, isn't she?' Reece gave a chuckle as he followed Luke's line of vision.

'I'm sorry?' Luke feigned ignorance, but Reece wasn't having any of it.

'Oh, come off it, man,' he said, 'you know exactly what I mean. I saw you yesterday when she came into the staffroom—positively drooling you were. No, don't deny it.' He laughed as Luke opened his mouth and they fell into step. 'I would have been the same myself a few years ago. I don't have the energy now.' He gave a deep wistful sigh. 'But a youngster like you... Mind you,' he added darkly, as they reached the steps to the front doors, 'I should watch your step if I were you.'

'What do you mean?' Luke frowned, wishing that Reece hadn't started this particular conversation. The last thing he wanted was for anyone to suspect the way he felt about Ellie before he'd had time to see where he stood with her.

'Well, she's married,' said Reece, and the bottom dropped out of Luke's world.

'What did you say?' He stopped and stared at Reece.

'She's married,' Reece repeated. 'I'm sorry, old man,' he said as he caught sight of Luke's expression. 'Didn't you know?'

'No.' Luke shook his head. 'I didn't know.' He paused. 'Are you sure?' he added.

'Positive,' said Reece cheerfully, 'so, like I said, watch your step. We don't want any irate husbands to contend with, do we?'

Married. So that was the explanation for her reaction on seeing him the day before. Five minutes later Luke was sitting at his desk, staring miserably at his blank computer screen. He supposed he wasn't really surprised. It seemed inevitable that a lovely girl like Ellie would have been quickly snapped up. He had no one to blame but himself. If he'd had any sense he would never have let her go, and if his career had been such an issue at that particular time he should have suggested that Ellie go to the States with him. And now it was too late. Too late he had realised that Ellie was the woman he wanted, and he had left it too late to come back to find her. In the meantime, some other man had realised how lovely she was and had made her his wife. There was little point now in trying to see her, trying to talk to her, trying to start again.

Somehow he managed to start his morning surgery and concentrate on the patients who brought him the usual variety of problems. The weather was still extremely hot and that in itself was the cause of a whole spate of ailments, from a child with heatstroke and another with sunburn, to an elderly woman unable to cope with the extreme heat and suffering from dehydration and a man driven to distraction from the effects of prickly heat.

'I will give you antihistamine tablets and cream and you should soon feel some relief.' Luke printed out the prescription and handed it to the patient, and it was after the patient had left his consulting room and he was washing his hands before pressing the buzzer for his next patient that there came a tap on the door. Before Luke had a chance to answer Reece put his head round the door.

'Reece?' Luke looked up sharply.

'Luke, old man, I made a mistake,' said Reece.

'A mistake?' Luke straightened up.

'Yes, our lovely new locum.'

'What about her?'

'Well, I told you she was married, didn't I?'

'Yes, Reece, you did.' Luke paused. 'Are you telling me now that she isn't?'

'Yes, I got it all wrong apparently. I thought William said she was married.'

'And he didn't say that?' Luke stared at him, hardly daring to believe what he was hearing.

'No, he didn't. What he did say was that she is a single parent.'

'A single parent?'

'Yes, apparently she isn't married but she does have a baby.'

'I see...' said Luke slowly. Suddenly he was aware of the lifting of the gloom that had settled over him since early that morning. 'A baby, you say...?'

'Apparently so. But like I say, she told William she's a single parent, which sounds like she's on her own, so who knows? You could still be in with a chance.' With a laugh Reece withdrew and shut the door of Luke's room.

Ellie wasn't married. He stood up and walked to the window, where he stood for a long moment looking at the busy market scene in the street below. She had a baby but she wasn't married. She was free. The baby, of course, meant that someone else had replaced him in her affections, but that was only to be expected. Four years was a long time and he could hardly have expected her not to become involved with anyone else in that time.

But a baby—how did he feel about that? It must

have been a pretty serious involvement to result in a baby. He frowned. Reece had seemed certain that she was on her own, so did that mean the baby's father had abandoned her—walked out when he'd heard about the baby, leaving her to cope alone? Luke felt his hands tighten into fists. How anyone could treat Ellie like that, he didn't know. But where did that now leave him? Would he still want to resume his relationship with Ellie, always assuming she would have him back, knowing that she had another man's child? And if things worked out between them, would he be able to treat that child as his own? The answer was there almost as soon as the question had formed in his mind—of course he would. He'd loved Ellie once, he should never have let her go, and if she would only give him the chance he would love her again.

Ellie had sensed that Luke had wanted to speak to her that morning when she had parked her car and she had been quite relieved when Reece had arrived and distracted him. She was dreading the moment when Luke would question her about what she had been doing with her life since he had left and although she knew that moment would surely come, she was also happy to delay it for as long as possible.

She'd had a bad night. Not only had it been so hot that she'd been unable to sleep, but when she had finally dropped off she had dreamt of Luke, of how it had once been between them, and she had woken quite shaken and longing for him. At one time he had been her whole world and she had loved him like she had never loved anyone before, but when it had become apparent to her that he simply hadn't been ready to make a commitment, she had reluctantly allowed him to move on out of her life.

Deep down she knew she'd never stopped loving him, a certainty that had been confirmed now that she'd seen him again. But now, because of Jamie, everything was different. He hadn't wanted to commit to her before so it was unlikely that he would now. If he found out about Jamie, and decided that he did now want commitment, surely that would be for the wrong reasons? It was why she hadn't told him about her pregnancy in the first place, so surely in that respect nothing had changed? Round and round the thoughts had whirled in her head and when at last it was time to get up for work she felt hollow-eyed and exhausted.

As she sat in Judy Maxwell's consulting room and waited for her first patient, she needed every ounce of her concentration. A knock on her door broke into her thoughts.

'Come in,' she called, and a heavily pregnant young woman came into the room.

'Hello.' Ellie glanced at the notes. 'I'm Dr Renshaw. It's Denise Tolley, isn't it?'

'Yes,' the woman replied and sank thankfully down onto the chair that Ellie indicated. 'I don't like this heat,' she said. 'It doesn't really go with pregnancy.'

'How far along are you?' Ellie pressed a couple of buttons on the computer and brought the woman's records onto the screen.

'Thirty-nine weeks,' Denise replied. 'Dr Maxwell and I were having a race to see who could give birth first—have you heard if she's had her baby yet?'

'Not as far as I know,' said Ellie with a smile. 'So, how may I help you today?'

'I'm suffering from terrible heartburn,' Denise replied, 'and at night I'm getting sciatica when I lie down.'

'Well, let's take the heartburn first,' said Ellie. 'Show me exactly where it is. When does it mainly occur?' she added as Denise indicated the area of the pain.

'Usually about half an hour after I've eaten and again, like the sciatica, as soon as I lie down at night.'

'When was your last antenatal check?'

'A few days ago,' Denise replied. 'I mentioned both these things to the midwife and she suggested I make an appointment to see you.'

'Right.' Ellie stood up. 'Let's just check on baby. If you'd like to go into the examination room and just take off enough so that I can listen to baby's heartbeat.'

A couple of minutes later Ellie joined Denise in the examination room and found her lying on the couch. 'I had a job to get up here,' Denise joked. 'Honestly, if I get any bigger I won't be able to waddle around.'

'This is your second baby, isn't it?' Ellie paused for a moment, looking down at Denise and the huge mound of her abdomen.

'Yes.' Denise nodded. 'I already have a little girl, Mollie, and this one's a boy—we're going to call him Sam. My husband's football-mad—he's already talking about buying him an England football strip.'

'So he's pleased, then?' said Ellie as she began to examine Denise gently in order to determine the baby's position.

'Oh, he's over the moon,' said Denise. 'Don't get me wrong,' she added hastily, 'Mollie is the apple of his eye and a proper little Daddy's girl, but this one, well, I guess all men want a son, don't they?'

'Er, yes…yes, I suppose they do.' Suddenly Ellie felt uncomfortable as she recalled how she'd felt the previous day when she'd taken Jamie to the park and it had dawned on her for the first time that not only had she deprived Jamie of a father's love and attention but she had also prevented Luke from knowing what it meant to have a child. To cover her discomfort she leaned over and listened to the baby's heartbeat. 'That's nice and strong,' she said at last, straightening up. 'What about movements?'

'Oh, all the time,' said Denise. 'Not quite so fierce as it was at one time.'

'That'll be because he doesn't have so much room now to take a really good kick,' said Ellie with a smile, 'but I'm pleased to tell you that the head is well down so he's getting into position to make his entrance. It shouldn't be too long now—any day really, I should think. If you'd like to get dressed and come back into the other room, I'll just check your blood pressure.'

Denise returned from the examination room and Ellie checked her blood pressure and reassured her that it was normal for her condition. 'Now,' she went on, 'I'll prescribe you a mild antacid to help with the heartburn but I'm afraid there's very little we can do about the sciatica—that, as I'm sure you well know, is due to the baby's position in that he's pressing on the sciatic nerve. Try surrounding yourself with pillows when you lie down, using them to support your back and hips.'

'OK, thank you.' Denise pulled a face. 'But it really is agony sometimes, trying to get comfortable.'

'I know,' said Ellie sympathetically, 'but at least you know it will soon come to an end.'

'Do you have children, Dr Renshaw?' asked Denise.

'Yes, I have one,' said Ellie, 'a little boy.'

'And how old is he?' asked Denise as she stood up and took the prescription form that Ellie handed to her.

'Oh, he's three now,' said Ellie as she escorted Denise to the door. 'Well, if I don't see you again before the birth, I hope all goes well.'

'Thank you, Doctor.' Denise smiled and nodded then she was gone.

As Ellie closed the door and returned to her desk it suddenly dawned on her that in an unthinking moment she had actually told Denise about Jamie. She really would have to be more careful if she wanted to keep his existence a secret from Luke. Not that Luke was likely to see Denise Tolley in the foreseeable future, and even if he did, Denise would hardly be likely to reveal details of the private life of one of his colleagues. She really would have to stop being so paranoid, Ellie told herself grimly, because if she didn't it was doubtful she would survive the next six months.

Gradually she worked through the rest of that morning's surgery. Most of Judy Maxwell's patients were quite happy to see her, some were openly curious and there were the inevitable few who were taking advantage of the opportunity for a second opinion.

When she had finished the list she saw a couple of extra emergency patients then visited two elderly housebound patients, one suffering from chronic arthritis and the other from Alzheimer's disease. By the time she had completed these house calls it was lunchtime and her shift was over for the day. As she left the building she decided to leave her car in the car park as she had several errands to do in the town, but she had barely shut the main doors behind her when a sudden shout from the car park caught her attention. She turned sharply and saw Luke crossing the park towards her. Her pulse began to race a little faster, as it seemed to do whenever she saw him, then almost immediately her heart sank a little as she wondered what he wanted.

CHAPTER FOUR

THE sun was melting the tar on the road and rising from the ground in a shimmering haze. In spite of the heat, Ellie looked as cool and fresh as she had that morning when she had arrived for work. With her blonde hair tied back from her face she was wearing a floral-patterned skirt with a hem that flared gently around her knees and a sleeveless white top with a little stand-up collar. As Luke walked towards her across the car park he had to fight a sudden and irresistible urge to gather her into his arms and kiss her. He would have done that once and she wouldn't have minded, would have welcomed it, in fact. Now it was a different matter. Heaven only knew how she would react now. A sudden mental picture came into his mind of Ellie with this other man, the one who had given her a baby, and he was forced to fight another urge—this time one of almost uncontrollable anger. Then he dismissed the image from his mind. If he was to make any headway at all with Ellie, he would have to control any such jealous tendencies. And he was jealous of this other guy, whoever he was—there was no denying that.

He cleared his throat, realising that Ellie was waiting for him to say something. 'Ellie,' he said, casually, he hoped, but feared inanely, 'I was hoping to see you.'

'Oh, yes?' she said, and he thought she seemed

wary which, under the circumstances, was probably true.

'Have you finished your shift for today?' he asked, aware that a trickle of sweat which he doubted had anything to do with the heat of the day was running down his neck and seeping into the collar of his shirt.

'Yes,' she said, and he marvelled afresh at how cool she looked. Her skin was lightly tanned, as soft and silky as a child's. He knew exactly how it felt to touch, could remember every detail of her, even down to the mole on her left breast and the tiny birthmark halfway between her right hip and her navel. But he mustn't think about that now, he thought in sudden desperation. If he did he would start acting like a complete idiot and drive her away once and for all.

'I was wondering,' he said, 'that is, if you don't have to rush off home straight away, if you'd like a bit of lunch...'

'Well, actually...' She glanced at her watch.

'It wouldn't be for long,' he said quickly, 'I have a surgery at two-thirty, but I do know a rather nice little place just round the corner from the Minster that does the most delicious hot cheese scones...' He knew she liked cheese scones, remembered an occasion when they had sat before a roaring log fire and eaten hot cheese scones with lashings of butter, and he saw now by her sudden, almost rueful little smile that she also remembered that occasion. That time they had ended up in bed together and the most glorious sex had followed. This time, no doubt, would be very different, but thank God for memories, he thought. Knowing she was still wavering, he went on, 'We needn't be long...unless, of course, there is somewhere else you need to be?'

'Er, no, not really.' Still she hesitated while Luke willed her to make up her mind and reach the right decision. 'I do have a few things to do in town before I go home—the bank, pick up some clothes from the cleaner's...' She took a deep breath and once again he had to almost physically restrain himself from leaning forward and kissing her mouth. 'Oh, all right,' she said at last, and Luke breathed a huge inward sigh of relief, 'but I really mustn't be too long.'

They walked to the little café situated in the shadow of the towering building of the Minster and sat down at one of the tables set outside beneath a striped awning. For Luke, just being with Ellie like that, walking side by side down the cobblestone lane then sitting together after the waitress had taken their order, it felt like they had never been apart and briefly, as he surreptitiously watched her, he wondered if she felt the same way. If she did she gave no indication and in the end he dared to voice his thoughts. With a deep sigh he leaned back in his chair, stretched and linked his hands behind his head. 'This is just like old times,' he said. She didn't answer and he threw her a sidelong glance. She was wearing sunglasses now and it was impossible to gauge her reaction to his statement. 'Ellie...?' he prompted at last.

'Yes?' Coolly she turned her head in his direction and the urge was back, this time to run his fingers down the back of her slender neck. In desperation, he seriously considered sitting on his hands.

'I said this was just like old times...' he repeated.

'Yes, I know, I heard you,' she said.

'And don't you agree?' He raised his eyebrows.

'Well,' she said consideringly, 'I guess it is, and it isn't...'

'Would you care to expand on that remark?' he asked with a laugh. Then, as the waitress arrived with their order, they were both distracted. Moments later, after they had spread the hot scones with butter and he had watched Ellie bite into hers before taking a mouthful of his own, he once again returned to the last topic of conversation. 'So are you going to tell me what you meant?' he said.

'I would have thought it was pretty obvious,' she said with a little shrug. 'Yes, it is like old times in that we are sitting together in a café having lunch, but it is nothing like old times in that we are now two different people and our lives have moved on.'

'How do you mean?' He wasn't prepared to let her off lightly.

'Well... In the past we were together, we were an item, now we are merely colleagues. I would say there's a whole world of difference.'

'We could soon remedy that,' he said lightly.

'No, Luke.' He was shocked at the sudden sharpness of her tone. 'I don't think so.'

'But—'

'No.' She held up her hand. 'I always think it's a mistake to try to go back—things can never be the same again.'

He wanted to ask her about the baby but somehow he couldn't quite find the words. Instead, he heard himself say, 'Is there someone else, Ellie?' He held his breath as he waited for her answer.

'No.' She shook her head. 'There's no one else.'

He let out his breath. So Reece had been right about one thing, she was indeed a single parent and was no longer in a relationship with the father of her baby. Well, that was something, it was a start. Even if she didn't want to know yet, maybe over a period of time he would be able to win her round. 'So there's no reason why we shouldn't be friends?' he said at last.

She shook her head. 'No,' she said, 'I suppose not.'

They were silent for a while as Ellie poured the iced lemon tea they had ordered, then in a further attempt at encouraging her to open up a little Luke enquired after her mother.

'She's well,' said Ellie.

'Is she still doing her illustrations?' he asked casually, thinking this might lead Ellie on to saying—as he presumed was the case—that these days her mother helped look after the baby.

'Yes, she is.' Ellie nodded. 'She's freelance these days but she gets more than enough work.'

'I liked your mum,' he said, taking a sip of his tea.

'You only met her a few times,' said Ellie quickly.

'I know, but I still liked her.' He paused. 'Did you tell her that you are working with me?'

He saw Ellie hesitate then she gave a little nod. 'Yes,' she said, 'I did mention it.'

'And?' he said when she fell silent.

'And what?'

'Well, what was her reaction?' he persisted.

'She…she was surprised,' she said at last.

'Correct me if I'm wrong,' he said wryly, 'but I got the distinct impression that not only did I like your mum but that she also liked me. Am I right?' He lowered his head slightly in order to look into Ellie's face, but her expression was still hidden behind the dark glasses. 'Ellie?' he prompted, when she remained silent.

She looked up with a little toss of her head, the gesture in itself making him want her all over again. 'You know very well she liked you,' she retorted, 'so stop fishing for compliments.'

He threw back his head and laughed. 'In the old days she always told me I was welcome to call in if I was in the area—maybe that would still apply now.'

'That was then,' said Ellie quickly. 'Like I said, times have changed and we've all moved on.'

'So are you saying times have changed so much that I would no longer be welcome in your mum's home?' Luke raised his eyebrows.

'I've no idea.' Ellie gave a quick, dismissive gesture.

'Maybe I should try it one day and see,' he said.

Abruptly Ellie stood up. 'I really must get on, Luke,' she said.

'So soon?' He looked up at her.

'Yes, I told you, I have things to do. This has been very...' She seemed to be searching for the right word. 'Nice,' she said weakly at last. 'Thank you for lunch.'

'I'll walk back with you,' he said, rising reluctantly to his feet.

'I have to go to the bank,' she said quickly.

'Yes, you said, and the dry-cleaner's. I'll wait for you.'

Together they left the café and walked slowly back up the narrow cobbled lane to the high street. It was still very hot. Some of the shops were closed for the lunch-hour, and the main road was very quiet, reminding Luke of siesta time in Mediterranean countries. When they reached the bank, Ellie went inside and Luke followed her in order not to have to wait in the sun. It had been good to spend some time alone with her, even if she was still wary of him, and he felt quietly confident that soon, if he went about things in the right way, that barrier of wariness would be broken down. They might even be able to get back to the way things had been before. As he waited for Ellie while she joined the short queue of customers at the counter, a man came in behind him. As he turned, he saw it was Ritchie Austin.

'Hello, there, Doc,' said Ritchie amiably.

'Hello, Ritchie.'

'Doesn't get any cooler, does it?' As Ritchie mopped his forehead, Luke noticed how red in the face he was. He was sweating profusely as, without waiting for an answer, he went and stood behind Ellie in the queue.

At least it was cooler in the bank than outside, thought Ellie as she left Luke by the door and crossed the tiled floor to join the other customers waiting at the counter. There was an elderly lady in front of her, and further down the queue, being served, Ellie saw Denise Tolley. It crossed her mind once again how uncomfortable it must be to be so heavily pregnant in such a heat wave—then the thought went out of her mind as she began reflecting on the time she had just spent with Luke.

It had been inevitable that he should want to see her and talk to her and, although she had already made up her mind to be cool towards him and not encourage him in any way, to her surprise she had found that she actually enjoyed being with him again.

Not that that should have any bearing on the decision she had made earlier, of course, concerning Luke and Jamie. That still stood, and she was more firmly resolved than ever that she was doing the right thing.

Luke's talk about visiting her mother had been a little worrying but she was sure it was all only talk and would not pose a real threat in any way to the life she had made for herself and her son. No doubt in time Luke would find someone else and she would be left in peace. She frowned at the thought of Luke finding someone else then gave herself a little shake. It was what she wanted, wasn't it? It would be the best thing that could happen.

She turned slightly and looked back at Luke as he stood inside the door. At the sight of him, as he smiled and exchanged a word with a man who had just come into the bank, her heart melted a little in spite of herself. He looked just like the old Luke, like he had always done when they had loved one another. His hair looked slightly damp from the heat, his face was tanned and when he smiled his eyes crinkled slightly at the corners in that way she remembered so well. But it was his eyes that fascinated her, had always fascinated her, that tawny gaze with more than a hint of amusement. Almost as if he sensed that she was looking at him, he turned that gaze on her now, and for a split second it was as if there was no one else present. Their gazes locked and held, and the years that had separated them seemed to melt away.

Later Ellie was unable to remember clearly the sequence of events that happened next. For years afterwards she was to wonder whether the intense heat of that day had contributed to the madness of desperate men. Likewise, the relative quiet of the midday hour, the few customers and the little traffic also seemed to play their part. But at the time, although everything happened so fast, it was as if the events were played out in slow motion.

She was aware of noise—the screeching of tyres on hot tarmac, the slamming of car doors followed instantly by a crashing sound as the doors were flung open and three figures—or was it four?—their faces flattened and distorted by stocking masks, hurtled into the bank. There were shouts as the men screamed at the customers and staff, ordering them to lie flat. She was aware of Luke moving forward towards her, of Denise in front of her, screaming and clutching her belly. She saw that the men carried guns, then Luke grabbed her, pushed her to the floor and fell on top of her, shielding her body with his own.

She couldn't see any more because Luke's arm was across her face, but she heard further shouts as the bank staff were ordered away from the counter, the sound of the heavy bank doors slamming shut, further screams from terrified customers and staff, then an ominous silence broken only by the sound of desperate sobbing.

'Luke…?' she whispered. 'What's happening?'

'Stay still,' he whispered back, 'perfectly still. I'll try and see.' That was as far as he got for at that moment more screams and yells ensued, followed by the ear-shattering sound of a gunshot. Deadly silence followed then more screams.

'Oh, my God,' whispered Ellie. 'Luke, what is it? What's happening?'

Cautiously Luke lifted his head. 'I think they've shot one of the bank staff,' he whispered. 'I think he tried to raise the alarm.'

'Oh, no,' whimpered Ellie. At that moment all she could think was that they might all be shot. Thoughts of Jamie flashed through her mind, and her mother, and in terrified desperation she clung to Luke, so safe and so comfortingly familiar, thankful that he was with her.

In the shouts and yells that followed it seemed that the gang were arguing with each other then they began yelling and shrieking obscenities at the customers who were still lying on the floor, telling them to get up and to throw any mobile phones onto the floor.

'We must do as they say,' murmured Luke as he helped Ellie to her feet and they threw their phones onto the floor. Together, at gunpoint, the customers were herded into a room behind the counters, which appeared to be some sort of storeroom. Ellie saw that between them the bank staff had half carried and half dragged their injured colleague into the room with them. When they were all inside the room the door was slammed shut behind them and they heard the sound of the key being turned in the lock. Immediately everyone's attention was on the man who had been shot.

'We are doctors,' said Luke, indicating himself and Ellie. 'Let us through, please.'

The bank employees moved back in relief as Luke and Ellie knelt beside the man.

'Is he dead?' asked a woman, hysteria in her voice.

Ellie looked at Luke as he felt for a pulse. 'No,' he said at last, and a sigh of relief rippled through the room, 'he's alive but he's unconscious.' While Ellie loosened the man's tie and unbuttoned the neck of his shirt, Luke lifted back his jacket and Ellie could see that pellets had peppered an area in his left shoulder, which was bleeding profusely. 'We need something to help stem the bleeding,' Luke said. The man who had been talking to Luke at the doorway of the bank immediately pulled off his shirt and handed it to Luke, who glanced up. 'Thanks, Ritchie,' he said, then fashioned it into a pad before holding it to the wound, exerting pressure to staunch the flow of blood.

'What do you think they are going to do with us?' It was Denise, predictably, in view of her condition, who voiced the question that must have been upper-most in everyone's mind.

'Once they've got what they came for, they'll go,' said Ritchie.

'Did Brian actually press the panic button be-fore…before…?' whispered one of the women who had been on duty at the counter.

'I don't know,' said another, 'I couldn't look…' As if in answer to the question, in the distance came the wailing sound of police sirens.

'He must have done,' said someone else, almost sobbing with relief. 'Oh, thank God. I thought…I thought they were going to shoot all of us.'

'Do you think they've gone?' asked the elderly lady who had been standing in front of Ellie in the queue.

Before anyone had the chance to voice an opinion there came the distinct sound of more gunfire.

'Oh, dear God, no!' cried Denise. 'Whatever is happening now?'

'I reckon the police arrived just as they were trying to make their getaway,' said Ritchie.

'Do you think they've caught them?' said another of the bank staff.

'We can only hope, love,' said Ritchie. Looking down at Luke and Ellie, he said, 'How's he doing?'

'He's losing a lot of blood,' said Luke. 'We need to get him to hospital.'

'Well, hopefully we'll be able to now,' said Ellie. 'Surely the police will have sent for ambulances.' She imagined that any moment the door to the storeroom would be flung open and they would be faced with the familiar, reassuring sight of uniformed police officers. But the minutes ticked slowly by and nothing happened, and all the while she and Luke struggled to stem the flow of blood from the man's shoulder wound.

'Do you think they know we are here?' asked the elderly lady at last.

'Well, they must have known there would be staff on duty,' said one of the counter staff.

'And presumably customers...' added Ritchie. 'Perhaps we should let them know we are here. What do you think, Doc?'

'Good idea,' said Luke. 'Make as much noise as you can.'

They needed no second bidding and within seconds they were hammering on the office door and shouting at the tops of their voices in the hope of attracting the attention of the police.

But after ten minutes of shouting and hammering, the door still remained firmly shut.

'I reckon we could break the door down,' said Ritchie at last.

'I doubt it.' It was a young man, one of the bank staff, who replied. 'That's a fire door. It's solid and the locking system in this place is second to none.'

'So what do we do?' asked Denise.

Ellie caught the desperation in her voice and she glanced up. 'Are you all right, Denise?' she said.

'I don't know. I'm not sure,' Denise replied. 'If I'm really honest, I'm not feeling too brilliant.'

Ellie stood up and crossed the room to Denise who was sitting on one of the room's two chairs. 'What is it, Denise?' she said quietly.

'I'm not sure.' Denise shook her head. 'I feel a bit faint.'

'It's probably the shock,' Ellie replied. 'Come on, put your head down—that's right. You'll soon feel better.'

'Why haven't they let us out?' One of the girls from the bank counter staff began to cry. 'I don't like it in here. I get very claustrophobic…'

Luke beckoned to Ellie to take over from him in keeping up the pressure on the gunshot wound. With a reassuring touch on Denise's shoulder Ellie did as he had bidden her. Luke stood up and everyone looked at him to see what he was about to say.

'I don't know why we haven't been released,' he said, 'but it can only be a matter of time before we are. In the meantime, we have to face a few facts.' He glanced round the room. 'There are eleven of us in this room and we have a man who is seriously injured, he has to be our top priority. There is very little we can do, but the one essential thing is that we all remain calm. Is that understood?' He looked round at the ring of silent faces then people began to nod. 'I don't suppose there is a telephone in here anywhere?' He glanced to the young man as he spoke.

The man shook his head. 'No, this is purely a store for stationery and office equipment and cleaning materials.'

'What's in there?' Luke indicated a door at one end of the room.

'Toilets, and at the other end is our staff kitchen,' the man replied.

'So at least we have facilities and presumably running water,' said Ellie.

'Shame about the mobile phones,' said Ritchie. 'At least we would have had contact with the outside world if they'd allowed us to keep them.'

'I kept mine,' said a voice from the corner of the room, and everyone turned to see who had spoken. It was the elderly lady who had been in front of Ellie in the queue.

'What did you say, love?' said Ritchie in amazement.

The lady was sitting primly on the second of the room's two chairs and was clutching her handbag. 'I kept my mobile phone,' she said calmly. 'My grandson gave it to me for my birthday and I was blessed if I was going to hand it over to those thugs. I've only just learnt how to use it,' she added proudly.

'Well, good for you, love,' said Ritchie in admiration while the others looked at her in something approaching awe.

'Yes,' said Luke, 'that was very brave of you.'

'Well, now that we've established the fact that we have access to a phone,' said Denise, 'don't you think it might be a good idea to use it and make contact with the outside world?'

'Good idea.' Ritchie chuckled. 'We don't want you having that baby before we get out of here, do we?'

As Denise looked at him in horror, Ellie silently hoped that wouldn't happen.

CHAPTER FIVE

'WHOM do I phone?' asked the lady. 'My son?'

'It might be better if you were to phone the police,' said Luke, as Ritchie gave a snort of exasperation.

'I want my son to know that I'm all right,' the lady replied stubbornly, but, catching sight of Ritchie's expression, she handed the phone to Luke. 'You do it,' she said. 'You'll be able to explain things better than me.'

Luke glanced at Ellie who was still kneeling beside the injured man. She looked white and shocked and after only a moment's indecision he dialled 999 and asked to be put through to the police. When the call was answered he identified himself then briefly went on to explain where he was and what had happened. He then waited while his call was transferred, all the while acutely aware that everyone in the room, with the exception of the injured man, was hanging on his every word and waiting in an agony of suspense to find out what was happening and why they hadn't been released.

At last his call was taken up by another centre and he was asked how many people were with him.

'There are eleven of us,' he replied, 'six bank staff and five customers. One of the staff has a gunshot wound and needs to be transferred to hospital as soon as possible. We also have a pregnant lady here.' He was then asked their exact location. 'We are locked in a storeroom at the rear of the bank— No, we didn't lock ourselves in, the gang herded us in here and locked the door— No, we haven't seen them since.' Luke was silent as he listened intently then, taking a deep breath, he said, 'Right. Yes. OK. But don't take your time, will you?' With that he pressed the 'end' button of the phone and looked at the expectant circle of faces around him.

'Well?' demanded Ritchie. 'What's happening?'

'Why haven't they let us out?' asked one of the bank employees.

'I hardly know how to tell you this,' said Luke, 'but it appears the raid went drastically wrong—from the gang's point of view, that is—and the police arrived before they made their getaway.'

'Well we'd more or less worked that out,' said Ritchie.

'Yes,' said Luke, 'but we were assuming that the police had rounded them up.'

'You mean they haven't?' It was Ellie who posed the question.

Luke shook his head. 'No,' he said, 'it appears the gang have barricaded themselves inside the bank.'

'What?' Ritchie gaped at him and as the truth of what he was saying sank in amongst the others a ripple of fear ran through everyone.

'You mean they are still in here with us?' whispered one of the bank employees.

'Yes, I'm afraid so.' Luke looked at Ritchie. 'You're thinking what I'm thinking,' he said, his gaze shifting to the door.

'Yes,' said Ritchie. 'If we could shift those filing cabinets, we could barricade ourselves in here—at least, that way we'd be safe from—' But that was as far as he got for at that precise moment the door was flung open and three of the gang, still with their faces contorted by the stocking masks and wielding sawn-off shotguns, burst into the room. There were screams from several of the women. One of the men stayed in the doorway with his gun trained on the occupants of the room while the other two began investigating the kitchen and toilets, presumably to see if there was any form of exit. They grew increasingly frustrated when it became evident that there was not.

In the end it was the elderly lady who had clung to her mobile phone who squared up to one of the men, the one standing guard in the doorway. 'You can't keep us here,' she said, her voice steady and impervious, as if she were dealing with a naughty schoolboy instead of a desperate, gun-wielding thug. 'We have an injured man here, and this man...' she indicated Luke '...is a doctor. He says he needs to go to hospital right away.'

The man in the doorway began yelling obscenities but was silenced by one of the others who swung round on Luke. 'You a doctor?' he demanded, his voice muffled and guttural behind his mask.

'Yes.' Luke nodded and the next moment he was being hustled from the room. As he went he was aware of Ellie's white face, her hand stretched out towards him in desperation, and vaguely he saw the terror on the faces of some of his companions. Then he was in the corridor and the door was being shut and locked again and in the company of the three thugs he was marched into a room which, with its desk, chairs and potted plants, was presumably the manager's office. A man was lying on the floor, his face still concealed behind a mask, a rapidly expanding pool of blood beneath him seeping through the denim of his jeans onto the carpet.

'Sort him out.' One of the men holding Luke pushed him forward. Staggering slightly, Luke knelt beside the injured man and attempted to assess his injuries. He was moaning softly and appeared to have been shot in the upper thigh. Reaching forward, Luke attempted to remove the man's mask. Immediately this action brought a torrent of abuse from two of the men watching.

'For God's sake, he needs air,' retorted Luke. The two men looked at the third man, who shrugged then indicated for Luke to continue. The injured man gave a great gasp as Luke peeled back the stocking mask and his face was uncovered, then he began to take several deep breaths. Luke was shocked to see how young he was, probably still in his teens, his skin without stubble, slightly spotty.

'Where am I?' he gasped. 'What's happening?'

'It's all right, son,' said Luke. 'You've been injured.'

'Who are you?' Wildly the boy looked at Luke then, looking up, his gaze travelled around the masked faces of his associates.

'I'm a doctor,' Luke explained. 'Hopefully we'll soon be able to get you to hospital where that bullet can be removed.'

'I...I've...been shot...?' gasped the youth incredulously.

'Yes,' Luke replied. 'It happens if you carry guns.'

'Shut it!' yelled one of the watching men, and Luke shrugged.

Looking up at his captors, he said, 'I need to clean this wound.' As he spoke his gaze fell on a bottle of mineral water on the desk. 'I'll have that,' he said, 'and I'll need scissors or a knife.'

'What for?' mumbled one of the men.

'To cut his jeans away from the wound.' Luke looked up sharply as one of the gang produced a flick knife and handed it to him with dire warnings, liberally peppered with further obscenities, about not getting any ideas. A knife wasn't the ideal implement to cut denim, but Luke managed as best he could, cutting the fabric away from the youth's leg and exposing the wound, which was still bleeding profusely. 'I need cloth of some sort,' he said as he unscrewed the top of the bottle.

Cloth, however, seemed to be beyond the resources of the gang so in the end Luke was forced to pull off his jacket and remove his own shirt, which, with the aid of the flick knife, he tore into strips. He soaked two of the strips with the water and attempted to cleanse the wound while the youth screamed in agony. 'Hold him still, please.' Luke looked up at the silent men then one of them put his gun onto the desk, knelt down beside the youth and held his arms.

'Don't do that!' yelled the youth. 'Vinnie, stop him!'

'No names!' yelled another of the men, thrusting his shotgun into the terrified youth's face. The yells gradually ceased replaced by loud groans as Luke cleaned the wound.

On closer investigation he found that the bullet had, in fact, shattered the youth's femur. He glanced up at the two men who were still standing guard over them. One, the thicker set of the two, appeared to be older than the others and quite possibly the leader. 'The bullet has lodged in the bone,' said Luke.

'Bastards!' spat the older man. 'Patch him up,' he ordered abruptly.

'I can't do much,' Luke replied.

'You're a doctor, aren't you?' growled the man.

'I have no equipment or medication with me,' said Luke with a shrug. 'Like the other injured man, he needs to be in hospital.'

'No hospitals,' muttered the man. 'Just patch him up,' he added after a further string of expletives.

'I need to stop the bleeding,' said Luke, looking around the office. 'Give me one of those cushions.' One of the men flung him a cushion from a chair and Luke ripped off the cover, folded it into a pad then covered it with some of the fabric from his shirt. He then pressed the pad over the wound and applied pressure. As he did so he nodded towards the bottle, which still contained some of the mineral water. 'Give him a drink,' he said. The man who had been restraining the youth turned his head then picked up the bottle and held it to the youth's lips. He gulped down the rest of the water.

After a while Luke lifted the pad but the wound was still bleeding profusely, the blood soaking into the surrounding carpet turning it from beige to red. 'This isn't working,' he muttered, half to himself and half to the watching men.

'Then do something else.' The older man emitted a stream of blasphemy.

Luke knew he had to stop the bleeding or the youth could bleed to death. He also knew the only other course of action open to him was to fashion a tourniquet. Turning back to what fabric was left from his shirt, he took the strip and twisted it to strengthen the fibres. Slipping the length beneath the youth's thigh, he tied the ends as tightly as he could. Almost immediately the blood turned to a trickle then just a faint oozing from the wound. Carefully Luke replaced the pad over the wound, securing it with a second, thinner strip of fabric, then he looked up at his captors. 'That's all I can do,' he said.

'Will he live?' grunted one of the men.

'Hopefully,' Luke replied. 'It depends how quickly he gets to hospital.'

'You've stopped the bleedin', haven't you?' demanded the older man.

'Yes,' Luke agreed calmly, 'I have, but I wouldn't recommend leaving that tourniquet on for any longer than is strictly necessary.' He took a deep breath. 'Likewise, the other injured man also desperately needs medical attention in hospital.'

'He's not our concern.' The older man spat on the floor.

'He will be if he dies,' said Luke, 'because that will be murder.'

'Shut it!' yelled the leader. 'If the pigs know what's good for them, they'll let us out of here. If they don't, there could be a few more bodies…!'

As the meaning of his words sank in Luke felt his blood run cold. Trying not to show any signs of fear or even agitation, he picked up his jacket and slipped it on.

'Where d'you think you're going?' sneered one of the gang.

'There is another man needing attention,' Luke replied.

'You can stay here until we know he's all right.' The older man jerked his shotgun in the youth's direction and Luke's heart sank. He had been counting on them taking him back to the others after he had tended their injured man to the best of his ability. He was desperate to get back to them to see what had happened in his absence, to see if the injured bank employee was stable. But more than anything he needed to see that no harm had come to Ellie and to let her know that he was all right. The one thing he was thankful for was that at the last minute, as the gang had burst into the storeroom, he had slipped the mobile phone into his trouser pocket. He could feel it there now as he sat down on the floor with his back to the wall. Its presence felt comforting but at the same time dangerous because this, their only link with the outside world, if detected by these thugs, could bring about a whole new spate of violence.

When Luke was frogmarched out of the room Ellie knew a moment of pure panic, panic because that effectively left her in charge of the seriously injured man, and panic over what their ultimate fate might be now that they knew they were holed up in the same building as the gang of gun-wielding thugs. But more than any of that, panic because she feared for Luke's safety. Why had they singled him out and taken him away? It had seemed to happen when they discovered he was a doctor, which perhaps indicated that one of their number had been injured or was ill. If that wasn't the reason she could hardly bear to contemplate what the real reason might be.

Keeping her fears to herself, she allowed her professionalism to take over as she continued to tend the injured man, keeping an eye on the wound for further signs of bleeding and making him as comfortable as possible with two jackets provided by his colleagues folded into a pillow and another to cover him.

'I know it's hot,' said Ellie, 'but because of the shock he's suffered he could soon become cold.'

'Does anyone know what happened to the phone?' asked the elderly lady hopefully.

'I saw the doc slip it into his pocket when that lot burst in,' said the young bank clerk, whose name turned out to be Spencer.

'Let's hope they don't find it,' said Ritchie darkly, and Ellie felt a further surge of fear for Luke at the hands of the gang.

'I want to phone my mum,' said one of the girls. 'She'll be worried sick.'

'She may not know about it yet,' said her colleague. 'She might still think you are at work.'

'Do you think they will just let us go?' asked Denise. 'I mean, why would they want to keep us here anyway?'

'We're their insurance,' said Ritchie with a short, derisive laugh, 'their safe passage out of here.'

'You mean like hostages?' Denise's eyes widened in horror and there was a stunned silence amongst the others.

'Well, I can't think of any other reason, can you?' said Ritchie with a shrug.

One of the girls began to cry and Ellie stood up, realising that without Luke and with the senior bank clerk lying injured at her feet she should assume some sort of lead if general panic was to be averted. 'We don't know that is the reason,' she said briskly. 'It may be something as simple as if they let us out, they could be letting the police in.' It didn't sound very convincing but it seemed to allay some of the fears of the two younger women and Denise, who was looking more agitated by the minute.

'I think,' she went on after a moment, 'that if we are going to remain in here for any length of time, we should at least know each other's names.' Looking round at the others, she said, 'I'm Ellie Renshaw and I'm a locum GP at the Oakminster practice with Luke—Dr Barron, that is.'

Further introductions followed as the others saw the practical nature of Ellie's suggestion. Of the bank counter staff the two younger women's names were Lizzie and Jo and their senior was Pauline. Of the office staff, apart from Brian Westwood, the injured man, and Spencer, there was a middle-aged secretary called Aileen Potter.

'And my name,' said the elderly lady, who had retained her mobile phone and who had so bravely faced up to the thugs, 'is Violet Calvert.'

'The next thing we need to do is to sort out our resources,' said Ellie.

'Do we have any?' asked Ritchie sceptically.

'Well, we know we have water,' Ellie replied.

'And that,' said Violet firmly, 'is the most important commodity of all.'

'Is there any food in the kitchen?' Ellie looked towards the bank clerks.

'Very little,' Lizzie replied. 'There might be a couple of packets of biscuits but that's about all. I'll go and have a look if you like.'

'Yes, please,' said Ellie. 'And if the rest of you could look in your bags or pockets to see what you have—sweets, that sort of thing—we'll pool everything to ensure that everyone gets something.'

'Surely you don't think we'll be in here that long,

do you?' Pauline stared at Ellie as if the potential seriousness of this new situation was just beginning to sink in. 'Won't the police just be able to break in?'

'They're dealing with armed men, don't forget,' said Ritchie, 'and presumably they have our safety to consider as well. Especially if our captors start bumping us off one by one…'

Jo screamed at his words and there were gasps from some of the others.

'I don't think we should start thinking along those lines,' said Ellie in a bid to avert further panic. 'Hopefully we won't be in here for too long, but as none of us have any means of knowing quite how long that will be we do need to draw up some sort of survival plan.' She glanced up as Lizzie came back from the kitchen. 'What do you have?' she asked.

'One packet of chocolate biscuits, one packet of rich tea biscuits and two chocolate bars,' Lizzie replied. 'There are about a dozen teabags, half a jar of instant coffee, some squash, a carton of milk and half a packet of sugar.'

'Well, it's better than nothing,' said Ellie. 'Now, did anyone have anything else? I have a packet of mints.' She placed the packet on the top of one of the storage cabinets.

'I have a packet of crisps and a tube of sweets.' Denise took the items from her bag and put them alongside the mints.

'I've got my lunch in my bag,' said Lizzie, and everyone looked at her. 'Trouble is, it's in the cloakroom.'

'Me, too,' said Jo, and there followed similar comments from the other members of staff. Violet Calvert had a small tin of cashews and Spencer had a packet of chewing gum in his pocket.

'Do you have anything, Ritchie?' asked Ellie.

'Nothing.' Ritchie shook his head. He had pulled on his denim jacket since losing his shirt to help staunch Brian's bleeding. 'I would have done,' he added. 'I always used to buy a couple of chocolate bars and maybe some crisps midday, but yesterday I saw Dr Barron and he told me I had to watch my diet. Sorry about that.' He looked round at the others. 'At least the doc will know I took notice of what he said.'

'That's if he ever comes back,' said Spencer gloomily.

'Of course he will,' said Ellie with more conviction than she was feeling. 'Now, in the meantime we've all had a shock so I suggest we all have a hot drink with plenty of sugar.'

It gave them something to do and for a short space of time took their minds off what might be happening elsewhere in the building. No one had suggested barricading themselves into the storeroom since the gang had taken Luke as it seemed everyone was of the opinion that he would be brought back when he had done whatever it was the gang required of him.

Lizzie and Jo boiled water in the kettle in the tiny kitchen and made tea and coffee. The biscuits were emptied into a tin and everyone was given one with a hot drink. These were taken in relays as there were only six mugs to drink from.

'The rest of the food we will have to ration out,' said Ellie. 'I suggest if we aren't released we have no more until early evening.'

'Oh God,' moaned Denise. 'I hope we get out before then.'

'Are you feeling all right?' asked Ellie.

'No, not really.' Denise shook her head. 'This sciatica is terrible and I'm still getting awful heartburn… I didn't even have a chance to pick up my prescription from the chemist.'

'What about your little girl?' said Ellie. 'Will she be all right?'

'She's with my husband,' said Denise. 'I wish I could phone them…'

'Maybe when Luke…Dr Barron gets back, you'll be able to.'

'That's if he still has the phone…or if he comes back…' Denise trailed off. She looked up at Ellie. 'What about your little boy?'

'My…?' Ellie stared at her then remembered that she'd told her about Jamie when she'd seen her earlier that morning in surgery. Had it only been that morning? It seemed like a week ago now with all that had happened. 'Oh, yes, Jamie,' she said. 'Luckily my mother will collect him from his nursery school, so I know he will be all right.'

'Do you think they know about us yet?' asked Denise.

'I should think so,' said Ritchie. 'It will probably have been on the local news by now, if not the national news.'

'My mum will be worried sick,' said Jo. 'I wish I could let her know I'm all right.'

'Trouble is, we don't know that we are all right yet, do we?' said Spencer. 'I mean, they could burst in here again any moment and mow us all down or, like Ritchie said, they could start bargaining with the police with us as the pawns. And if the police don't give 'em what they want, well…' He drew one finger across his throat.

'Shut up, Spencer,' said Aileen. 'You're just frightening everybody with talk like that.'

'I'm worried about my cat,' said Violet suddenly. 'He's shut in the house and he'll get very agitated if he isn't fed on time.'

No one made any comment about it being only a cat for it seemed that everyone's fears and anxieties were equally important in the frightening situation they found themselves in.

'May I suggest that we hide what food we have left?' said Pauline suddenly, and everyone looked at her. 'I mean…those…men won't have anything to eat either, will they? So if they discover we have something, they will be bound to grab it.'

'They might find our lunch,' said Jo, looking at Lizzie.

'I think yours is a good idea, Pauline.' Aileen hauled herself to her feet and disappeared into the kitchen. Moments later she returned. 'I've hidden the tin in the cupboard under the sink with all the cleaning materials. Hopefully, they won't think of looking there.'

'I wish they'd bring Dr Barron back,' said Violet. 'What do you think they could have wanted with him?'

'I reckon one of them was injured in that shooting we heard,' said Ritchie.

At that moment there came a low moaning sound from the man on the floor and Ellie, who was kneeling beside him periodically checking his pulse, turned to look at him. She was in time to see his eyes flicker open. 'Hello, Brian,' she said gently.

His eyes were blank as he stared up at her. 'Where am I?' he said at last.

'You're in the storeroom at the bank,' Ellie replied. 'Do you remember what happened?'

Briefly he closed his eyes again and his forehead became furrowed as he strove to remember. 'There was a raid...' he said at last. 'I...I pressed the alarm button...'

'Yes, Brian, you did,' Ellie agreed. 'You called the police, but you've been shot, Brian.'

'My God, yes.' He seemed to shudder as his memory must have flooded back.

'You passed out, but fortunately my colleague Dr Barron was in the bank—he tended to you.'

'And you...?' murmured a bemused Brian. 'Who are you?'

'Ellie Renshaw. I'm a doctor as well, and I work with Dr Barron.'

The man was silent for a few moments then, as he assembled his thoughts into some sort of order, he glanced around him at his colleagues and the others. 'Why...why are we in here?' he said at last.

Ellie took a deep breath. 'The...gang locked us in here,' she said at last.

'I don't understand...' he muttered. 'The police...?'

'There was a shoot-out,' Ellie explained.

'So...are you saying they are still here...?' Ellie saw the fear in his eyes.

'Yes.' She nodded. 'But I'm sure the police will get in soon. I want you to try and relax in the meantime.'

'Ellie! Dr Renshaw!' Ellie looked up sharply and saw Denise clutching her stomach.

'Denise?' she said urgently. 'What is it?'

'It's the baby…' Denise whispered. 'I think it's started.'

CHAPTER SIX

LUKE was sitting on the floor with his back against the wall, his knees drawn up and his wrists resting on his knees. The injured youth was less vocal than he had been, just muttering to himself from time to time. Luke thought he was slipping into delirium, fearing that in spite of his efforts to save his life he might not pull through. He found himself thinking what a waste that would be of a young life, a young life that had gone so drastically wrong.

The other gang members had not bothered to replace the youth's stocking mask after Luke had finished tending him, and Luke wasn't certain whether that was a good or a bad sign. Good for the youth certainly, but maybe bad for him. Perhaps it no longer mattered if Luke could identify him because Luke wouldn't be getting out anyway.

He had even heard the youth's name, along with the 'Vinnie' that had inadvertently slipped out when one of the gang had been restraining him. It had come later when the gang had been talking amongst themselves and had obviously thought Luke hadn't been listening, but he had heard it quite clearly, and now knew that the youth's name was Ross. He wondered about him, how he had become involved with the gang, thinking that maybe he was related to one of the others. Was that how criminals worked, drawing their recruits from their own families? Certainly the one called Vinnie had seemed more concerned about the lad than the others, which led Luke to wonder if Ross was his son or perhaps his brother.

He wondered about Ellie and the others in the storeroom and he wondered about the police outside and whether or not they would attempt to storm the building. If they did there would almost certainly be more casualties. He shuddered at the possibility, the thought that Ellie could be injured or even killed. Surely fate couldn't be so cruel, that no sooner had he found her again than she would be taken away from him.

On the other hand, maybe he would be killed and Ellie would survive—that would be preferable. But would she regret that they'd only just met again and not had the chance to resume any sort of relationship? Or was she not even thinking on those lines? She must be worried sick about her baby, he thought, and at the thought of that his mind began going off down the avenue of the relationship that Ellie must have had with the baby's father. Of course, it could have been a casual relationship or even a one-night stand, but that definitely wasn't Ellie's style. Ellie would have wanted commitment, which meant she had been very close to this guy, whoever he was.

Ellie had wanted commitment from him once. He could see that now, so why hadn't he been able to understand that at the time? Why on earth had he ever let her go? But let her go he had, and had sent her straight into the arms of this other man, the one with whom she'd had a baby. It didn't seem as if she was still with him, she herself had said there was no one else, but could he be sure?

Round and round the thoughts chased each other in his brain until at last he became aware that the gang

members were talking amongst themselves again and
he strained his ears to listen. He heard them complain
of being hungry and thirsty. He heard them arguing
about how to get out. And then he realised that one
of them—the older man—was in conversation with
someone on a mobile phone. He heard him setting
out some sort of demands—a fast car with a tankful
of petrol. He heard him mention those who were being held prisoner, including a pregnant woman, an
injured man and one of the town's doctors. Obviously
all this was being used as some sort of bargaining
tool and Luke sent up a silent prayer that they didn't
seem to know that Ellie was also a doctor.

The man came off his phone after that and further
arguing ensued. One wanted to simply make a run for
it and shoot their way out, another to use their pris-
oners as hostages, even killing some of them if need
be. Only Vinnie seemed concerned about the youth,
Ross, and how he would get away in his condition,
leading Luke to further speculate that he was a relative.

Eventually their talk turned to food again and Luke
realised that he too was thirsty if not exactly hungry.
A surreptitious glance at his watch told him that it
was five-thirty, which meant they had now been held
captive for four hours. Eventually the older man came
across to him and demanded to know if there was
food in the storeroom, but Luke was forced to admit
he had no idea.

Moments later he saw two of the men leave the
room, leaving the third to guard him and presumably
to watch over the injured man on the floor. He
strained his ears to listen, hoping that when they
opened the storeroom door he might hear some-

thing—anything—from those inside. But there was nothing and the next thing he knew one of the men came back.

'Get up!' he growled at Luke, sticking the two barrels of his sawn-off shotgun in his face. Luke needed no second bidding and scrambled to his feet. Once again he was marched at gunpoint down the corridor and when they reached the closed door of the storeroom the man jabbed him in the back with the gun. 'Get in there,' he muttered. 'You're needed—some crazy cow is having a baby.'

When Ellie heard from Denise that she thought the baby was coming, she knew a moment of utter helplessness. Doctor she may be, but was mere knowledge enough in this situation? How would she cope without any medical equipment or drugs and with only the most basic of facilities? She wished Luke were there. Why hadn't he come back? How would she cope if anything had happened to him? If the last few hours had taught her anything, it was just how much Luke meant to her, in spite of her having convinced herself otherwise. Then almost immediately the moment of helpless panic passed, and once again her professionalism took over.

'Are you having contractions?' she asked Denise.

Denise nodded. 'I have had pain low down in my back ever since we were pushed in here, and now the contractions are starting.'

'Oh, great,' said Ritchie with a snort. 'That's all we need.'

'Shut up.' Aileen shot him a furious glance. 'I'm sure the poor girl can do without comments like that. She needs our help.'

'OK.' Ritchie threw up his hands in a defensive gesture. 'What would you like me to do? Nip down to the chemist and get some nappies?'

At his words, facetious as they might have been, the seriousness of this new situation seemed to sink in. Pauline turned to Ellie. 'What would you like us to do?' she said.

'I want to examine Denise,' Ellie replied, 'so if you could give us some space here.' At Ellie's bidding, Spencer, Ritchie, Violet and the two younger women squeezed into the kitchen, leaving Pauline kneeling beside the injured Brian, watching for further signs of bleeding and Aileen to help Ellie with Denise.

After washing her hands carefully, as best as she could in the confined space of the storeroom, Ellie examined Denise and found that her cervix had started to dilate and she was indeed in the first stages of labour.

'Oh, what are we going to do?' Denise began to sob quietly as the enormity of the situation finally dawned on her.

'It'll be all right,' Aileen hastened to reassure her. 'We have the doctor here...'

'Yes, I know,' Denise choked, 'but what about afterwards? What about the baby...?'

'Let's just take one thing at a time, shall we?' said Ellie calmly. 'Your labour could take some hours and by then maybe all this will be over...the police may have got in by then.'

'Do you think,' said Pauline suddenly from her corner, where she sat beside Brian, 'it would do any good letting them—the gang, I mean—know about Denise and the fact that her baby is imminent?'

'Appeal to their better nature, you mean?' said Aileen.

'I doubt they have a better nature,' said Ellie, 'not men who go around shooting innocent people with sawn-off shotguns. 'But I see what you're saying and I suppose it might be worth a try…that is, if we see them again,' she added.

For the next hour or so Ellie sought to keep Denise as calm and as comfortable as possible. During that time everyone else fell silent, each of them conserving their energy for what they might have to face, contemplating what had happened and what might yet happen. At one point Denise even seemed to doze off between contractions and Ellie, sitting beside her on the floor, rested her head against the wall and closed her eyes.

Her thoughts inevitably turned to Jamie. While she feared the outcome of this situation, she knew, because of her mother's devoted care, that she had no immediate cause to worry about her son's welfare. Her son. Hers and Luke's, the only difference being that she knew she had a son and Luke didn't.

Should she have told him? If not at the time then when they had met again? Had her mother been right over this? Was it Luke's right to be told that he had fathered a son? She hadn't thought so, but had her motives been purely selfish? Had they been because she feared the consequences, possible access rights?

Maybe she had, but that had been when life had been relatively simple. This was now, and who could have ever in a million years have predicted the way their lunch-hour would have ended? Now, with lives hanging in the balance, did Luke have a greater right to know that he had a son? Would the knowledge make him all the more determined to survive this ordeal in order to meet and get to know his son, or would it render him full of helpless anger, and maybe make him careless? And all this was supposing that he returned to them, that he was even still alive.

Ellie shifted her position as anguish encircled her heart in a vice-like grip. He had to be alive. She couldn't bear it if he had been killed.

Her thoughts began to drift and she found herself remembering the time they'd first met. He had strolled onto the hospital unit one morning where she had been working, cool and casual in his white coat, stethoscope draped around his neck and with that dangerous glint in those tawny eyes that she had subsequently come to know so well. His gaze had fallen on her immediately and although no words had been spoken, that locked glance had been sufficient for him to seek her out later that evening at the hospital social club.

'Hi, there,' he said, walking straight up to her as she stood at the bar with a group of her friends. 'We met earlier but I didn't catch your name.'

She didn't correct him, tell him that they hadn't, in fact, met because by then she had already started to melt in the heat of that delicious tawny gaze. 'I'm Ellie,' she said weakly instead. 'Ellie Renshaw.'

'Luke,' he replied, reaching out his hand, taking hers and holding it between both of his almost as if he intended never letting her go. 'Luke Barron.'

There was no denying that the attraction or the chemistry between them was instantaneous and they began dating immediately. She was warned by other members of staff that he had a reputation as something of a heartbreaker.

'Watch him, Ellie,' her friend Lou said. 'I've heard he's of the ''love 'em and leave 'em'' variety. I know he looks good enough to eat but I don't want you getting hurt.'

She tried to exercise caution at the start, but within no time at all she had fallen head over heels in love with him and caution was thrown to the winds. She was already in far too deep by the time she learned he was going to the States to work, and for her own sanity, knowing he wanted no form of commitment, that he dreaded being tied down in any way, she was the one to try to cool things between them, to end the relationship before he went. And then, when she was still trying to get over losing him and facing life without him, then came the devastating discovery that she was pregnant. She bit her lip now as she thought about that time, and a couple of tears slid from beneath her eyelids and trickled down her cheeks. Without opening her eyes, she reached up her hand and brushed them away.

As afternoon turned to evening and the captives all seemed to have sunk into a stupor, the door to the storeroom was suddenly flung open again and they were confronted by two of the gang once more. Ritchie, with Spencer behind him, immediately came out of the kitchen and confronted the men, who both still wore masks and carried guns.

'Right, what's going on?' demanded Ritchie. His voice sounded authoritative, belligerent even, but Ellie detected a slight tremor that betrayed his fear.

One of the men yelled and swore at Ritchie and Spencer while the other crashed his way into the kitchen. They appeared to be searching for something and Ellie guessed it was food, hoping against hope they wouldn't find the biscuits hidden amongst the cleaning materials. They appeared to be about to leave again but at that point something seemed to snap inside Ellie and she drew herself up to her full height and faced the pair of thugs.

'How much longer do you think you're going to keep us in here?' she demanded. She seemed to take both men by surprise for they stopped in their tracks. 'We have a woman here who is about to give birth to a baby.' As if on cue, Denise suddenly gave a huge groan and clutched her stomach. 'She will need urgent medical attention. And while we're on that subject,' Ellie went on, her eyes flashing, seemingly for the moment oblivious to the precariousness of her position, 'what have you done with Dr Barron?'

One of the men uttered a string of obscenities and, lifting the butt of his shotgun, attempted to push Ellie out of the way. This seemed to incense Ritchie, who lunged forward, only to be struck in the face by the second thug, the impact throwing him across the room. With a cry Ellie's hand flew to her mouth and the door slammed shut once again behind the men. 'Oh, Ritchie.' Ellie put one arm around him as he stood winded, slumped against the wall. 'Are you all right?'

'Yeah,' he muttered. 'Take more than that to finish me off.'

'Well, sit quietly for a few minutes and get your breath back,' said Ellie. Looking through the doorway into the kitchen, where the others were herded together in the confined space, she said, 'Did they look in the cupboard under the sink?'

'They most certainly did,' said Violet. 'They looked everywhere.'

'Oh, no,' said Ellie. 'I suppose they found the biscuits and sweets?'

'Oh, no, they didn't,' said Violet. 'I'd thought about it and I figured that might be one of the first places they might look so I took the tin out.'

'What have you done with it?' asked Ellie.

'I'm sitting on it,' said Violet.

'Violet, that is very brave of you,' said Ellie weakly.

'Not at all,' said Violet briskly. 'I come from the generation who fought Hitler and his mob, it'll take more than this lot to frighten me, I can tell you.'

The fact that Luke hadn't been with the men caused Ellie to become more fearful for his safety than ever. 'I hope they haven't harmed him,' she said to Denise, voicing her fears as she began massaging the pregnant woman's back.

'Why would they?' muttered Denise. 'What possible motive could they have for harming a doctor?'

'Unless they're bargaining with his life,' said Aileen suddenly.

'What do you mean?' asked Pauline, looking up from the floor where she was wiping Brian's forehead as he showed signs of becoming agitated again.

'Ten years ago my brother was in an aircraft that was hijacked,' said Aileen. 'All the passengers and crew were taken hostage. They were on the runway for days and the first thing the hijackers did was to find out who they had aboard—anyone who was high profile, that sort of thing—to increase their bargaining power.'

'So you think that's what they might be doing with Dr Barron?' asked Pauline, her voice full of dread.

'Who knows?' Aileen shrugged. 'It was just a thought.'

'You could be right, though,' said Pauline. Looking at Ellie, she went on, 'In which case I don't think we should advertise the fact that Ellie is also a doctor.'

'I wonder if we have anyone else who is high profile,' mused Aileen.

'How about Ritchie?' muttered Denise between contractions.

'Nah.' Pauline shook her head. 'On the other hand, maybe he's a politician…'

Aileen nodded. 'Yes, and Violet could be a secret agent…'

The unexpected joking momentarily lightened the tension and brought smiles to the women's faces, but their relief was short-lived. Just as a further contraction seized Denise, the door was flung open again—and this time, to Ellie's utter relief, it was Luke who was pushed forward into the room by two men who accompanied him.

'Luke!' In a purely involuntary movement, and before anyone could stop her, she almost fell across the space between them and into his arms. 'Oh, Luke,' she choked, 'I thought…I thought… Oh, I don't know what I thought…'

'It's all right, Ellie,' he murmured, 'I'm here.' His arms tightened around her and in spite of the high tension of the moment all Ellie could think was how good it felt to be in his arms again, to be so close that she could hear his heart beating and feel the warmth of his skin. His skin… She looked down and realised he was only wearing his jacket and that underneath it his chest was bare. 'Your shirt…?' she said.

'It's a long story,' he replied grimly, glancing over his shoulder as the men backed out of the room and slammed the door shut again. They clearly heard the sound of the key turning again in the lock.

'They didn't have any plans to let us go, then?' said Pauline.

'That's the last thing they intend doing,' Luke replied. 'We are their ticket out of here.'

'But surely the police aren't just going to let them walk away?' said Ellie.

'They seem to think they will, rather than risk the lives of all of us,' said Luke.

Ellie realised he was still holding her and suddenly, embarrassed, she pulled away from him.

'What's been happening in here?' Luke looked around, his gaze coming to rest on Brian then moving to Denise. 'They seemed to think you are about to give birth,' he added.

'They're probably right there,' Aileen replied. 'Is that why they let you come back?' she asked curiously.

'I guess it must have been,' said Luke. 'I don't think they know Ellie is a doctor, which is just as well, and I suppose one of them may have had a sudden spark of humanity. Perhaps he has a wife who's just had a baby—who knows?'

'Why did they take you away?' asked Ellie curiously.

'One of them had been shot,' Luke replied, 'and they couldn't stop the bleeding. He's only a young guy, barely out of his teens.'

'Were you able to stop the bleeding?' asked Ellie. To her horror she found that she had started to shake

as the relief that Luke hadn't come to any harm began
to finally sink in.

'Only with a tourniquet,' he replied. 'I told them
he needed hospitalisation but I don't think they were
about to risk their own necks by ringing for an ambulance. How's our friend Brian?' Luke looked down
at the man on the floor.

'He's OK,' Ellie said. 'He came round briefly and
couldn't quite believe what had happened, but I think
he's drifted off again—isn't that right, Pauline?'

'Yes.' Pauline looked up. 'I gave him a couple of
sips of water but you're right—he seems to have
dozed off again.'

'And Denise?' Luke looked at Ellie.

'She's well under way,' Ellie replied, and as if to
confirm her words Denise was racked with another
contraction.

'We should do some sort of check on resources,'
said Luke.

'We've done that,' muttered Ritchie from the
kitchen doorway, a curiously subdued Ritchie since
the blow he'd received from one of the thugs. 'It's
biscuits and mints all round.'

'Really?' Luke raised his eyebrows.

'That's about it,' Ellie replied, 'but it's better than
nothing, and at least we have running water. Everyone
had a hot drink some while ago and a biscuit. I think
you should have the same, Luke.'

'I'll make it for him,' called Jo from the kitchen.

'Does that young man still have my phone?' called
Violet.

'Remarkably, yes,' Luke replied. 'Maybe it's time
we made contact with the outside world again, but
first I think it would be a good idea if we were to

carry out our original plan and try and barricade ourselves in here.'

With the help of Ritchie and Spencer Luke dragged
the two heavy filing cabinets across the storeroom and
positioned them in front of the door. Jo appeared with
his mug of tea and biscuit and he sat down on the
floor and took Violet's mobile phone out of his
pocket.

Ellie watched him as he dialled a number, and reflected that she'd never been so pleased to see anyone
in her life as she had when Luke had come into the
room. She really didn't know what she would have
done if anything had happened to him. The thought
was almost too awful to contemplate—a world without Luke not somewhere she wanted to be.

Everyone listened intently as Luke talked to the
police. Moments later he looked up at the circle of
faces around him.

'Well?' said Aileen, speaking for them all. 'What's
happening?'

'It's as we feared,' Luke replied, his face grim.
'They are trying to use us as bargaining tools for a
safe passage out of here. It seems they've asked for
a car and intend taking one or two of us with them
as hostages. If the police don't comply with that, they
say they intend using more drastic measures...'

'Oh, God, no!' cried Lizzie. 'They will kill us all
one by one.'

'Don't be ridiculous, girl,' said Violet sharply.
'Pull yourself together. They have to get in here first
and I think that might now prove to be a bit of a
problem.'

'That's what I told the police,' said Luke. 'I said
we've managed to barricade ourselves in.'

'Did they have any other advice for us?' asked Ellie.

'Just to sit tight,' Luke replied.

'I still think they'll storm the place,' said Spencer. 'You know, riot shields, helmets and rifles, the lot.'

'Well, let's hope they don't take too long about it,' said Aileen, glancing anxiously at Denise, 'otherwise they'll have twelve of us to rescue instead of eleven.'

CHAPTER SEVEN

THE next two hours seemed to pass remarkably quickly for Ellie, taken up as they were with helping Denise through her labour, trying to keep Brian as comfortable as possible and ensuring that any rise of panic amongst the others was quelled as soon as it began.

'You're doing well, Denise,' she said, after examining the woman again. 'I can see the baby's head now.'

'Oh, I didn't want him to be born under these conditions,' moaned Denise softly.

'He'll be just fine,' said Ellie, with more reassurance than she was feeling.

'But what if they get in here again?' Denise gripped Ellie's hand tightly as she attempted to ride another contraction.

'They won't,' Ellie replied firmly. 'Those filing cabinets are huge—it would take a battering ram to break through them and that's one thing I don't think our friends have.'

'But that's not all, is it?' gasped Denise. 'When my little girl was born she needed oxygen—what if this one's the same? And…and…what about the cord? How will you cut the cord?'

'You mustn't worry about any of that.' Luke leaned over and answered her questions. He had been attending to Brian and must have overheard Denise's fears. 'There's no reason to suppose that your baby

93

won't be anything other than fit and healthy when he's born. And as for cutting the cord, well, Violet has come up trumps once again and produced a pair of scissors from her handbag. Pauline is boiling water to sterilise them.'

This seemed to satisfy Denise, at least for the time being, and she sank back in exhaustion.

While Ellie and Luke were occupied with their patients Violet phoned her son and gave him strict instructions to feed her cat, then passed her mobile phone around so that everyone was able to make one call to their loved ones. 'Keep it brief,' Luke warned. 'If the batteries run out, we've lost our link with the outside world.'

'When did you last charge the batteries, love?' Ritchie looked at Violet, who shook her head.

'I didn't know I had to,' she said blankly, and there were groans from the others.

Ritchie phoned his wife and tried to calm her down. 'Anyone would think it's her being held hostage,' he muttered as he ended the call and passed the phone on.

Jo and Lizzie both phoned their mothers and tried to reassure them that they were all right. 'We've barricaded ourselves in the storeroom,' Jo explained breathlessly. 'We're just waiting for the police to come and let us out.' She paused. 'No, Mum, they're not going to kill us—they can't even get in to us. Don't take any notice of what you've heard on the news. Yes, I know. I love you, too, Mum.' With tears streaming down her cheeks, Jo passed the phone to Aileen.

After Pauline and Aileen had phoned their husbands and Spencer his mother, the phone was handed to Ellie. 'Your turn,' said Luke, his steady gaze meeting hers.

'Yes, right.' His gaze unnerved her slightly and she was uncertain quite what she could say to her mother in these exceptional circumstances.

Barbara answered immediately. 'Ellie?' she said, not waiting for Ellie to speak.

'Yes, Mum, it's me.'

'Oh, thank God! Are you out?'

'No, not yet, but listen, Mum, I only have a minute. I wanted you to know that I'm all right...'

'But it said on the news that you are all being held hostage—is that true?'

'Up to a point,' Ellie replied guardedly. 'We are in the bank—and the gang are also in here, but we've managed to barricade ourselves in a storeroom. It can only be a matter of time before the police get in. Now, quickly, is Jamie all right?' As she spoke she was suddenly very aware of Luke, who had turned away from her to tend to Brian again but who nevertheless would have heard every word she'd said.

'Yes, darling, of course he is,' her mother replied. 'Ellie, darling, I'll see you soon.'

'Yes, Mum, of course you will.' She didn't, couldn't, say goodbye. Instead, she said, 'Give Jamie a kiss for me.' She hung up and passed the phone to Denise. Luke still had his back to her. 'Do you want to phone your husband?' she asked.

'I don't think so.' Denise shook her head. 'If he knows the baby is coming he'll worry even more. Maybe I'll wait a bit...'

'OK.' Ellie took the phone and passed it to Aileen to return to Violet.

'You spoke to your mum?' asked Denise as Ellie turned back to her.

'Yes,' Ellie replied, 'I did.'

'And Jamie, is that your little boy?'

Ellie nodded, suddenly unable to speak. Luke still hadn't turned but she was sure he was listening.

'I think that's a lovely name—Jamie. I would have liked it for this one but my husband is adamant that we call him Sam...' Denise trailed off, her breath catching in her throat as a further contraction suddenly gripped her. 'Oh, God,' she muttered, 'here we go again!'

With the exception of Ellie and Luke and the injured man, who had once more drifted into unconsciousness, the others all crowded into the kitchen, leaving Denise some comparative privacy to give birth to her baby.

In the end it was a relatively easy birth and Ellie found herself thankful that this was Denise's second baby and not her first. 'At least there's no need for an episiotomy,' she said quietly to Luke as the baby's head was born. 'Right, Denise, I want you to pant for me now,' she said. 'Short, sharp breaths. You remember how you did it last time—yes, that's right, just like that. We don't want baby being hurtled into the world too fast, do we?'

'And what a world!' gasped Denise.

'Just think of the stories he'll be able to tell when he's older,' said Luke, 'about the drama of his birth and the incredible entrance he made.' Even as Denise was giggling weakly at Luke's comments, there came a commotion from the other side of the door behind the filing cabinets, the sound of loud shouts followed by thuds then a systematic thumping.

'Oh, my God,' moaned Denise. 'What's happening?'

'They've just discovered they can't get in,' muttered Luke as the filing cabinets began to shake under the onslaught on the storeroom door. At a further word from Luke, Ritchie and Spencer came into the storeroom and joined him, and together they put their combined weight against the cabinets.

As the three men struggled to maintain the barricade they had erected Ellie delivered Denise's baby.

When the battering had subsided and there was silence once more in the corridor outside the storeroom, Luke turned from the filing cabinets. As he caught sight of Ellie with the baby cradled in her arms he was suddenly overwhelmed by a great surge of tenderness, which just for a moment left him speechless. Then Ellie looked up and met his gaze. 'He's fine,' she said simply, reading the question in his eyes, the question he had been unable to put into words. 'He's just perfect.' Gently she took the baby's tiny hand, watching as his fingers encircled, then gripped one of her own.

'I still think it's a miracle, every time it happens,' said Luke, his voice suddenly husky with emotion. 'And this little one's entrance has an extra touch of the miraculous about it.'

'You can say that again,' said Ellie, her own voice suddenly shaky.

'And how's his mum?' Luke's gaze left Ellie and sought Denise.

'Yes.' Denise managed a smile and a thumbs-up sign. 'I'm OK as well.'

Pauline imparted the news to the others in the

kitchen and a loud cheer went up which, considering the circumstances they were in, brought tears to Denise's eyes. As if by some further miracle, Aileen had found some clean teatowels in a drawer in the kitchen and these were now put to good use, one to wrap the baby in, others for washing and drying both Denise and her son and, following the delivery of the placenta, one to wrap it in, in readiness for examination when they finally reached hospital.

'How is the blood loss?' asked Luke as Ellie examined Denise.

'Just moderate,' Ellie replied.

'Thank heavens for that,' said Luke as they both reflected on the problems they would have had if Denise had suffered a postpartum haemorrhage.

Following the excitement of the birth, and while Denise phoned her husband, Luke glanced at his wristwatch and saw that it was past eight o'clock in the evening. It was still very hot and the air in the storeroom and kitchen was becoming foetid and increasingly stale. 'I think,' he said to Ellie as she passed the baby to his mother, 'it's time to make more drinks and to eat something.'

'You're right,' Ellie said. 'I'll ask someone to organise that.'

He watched her walk into the kitchen. He wanted to ask her about her baby, but didn't know how to broach the subject, not here in front of all these people, in these dreadful conditions. He'd heard her on the phone to her mother, had heard her ask about Jamie, which presumably was the baby's name. He had caught the note of anguish in her voice and had recognised what agony she must be going through at the dreadful possibility that she might never see him again if things went drastically wrong in the hours ahead. He'd used his call to phone the police once again, knowing his own family were out of the country and probably wouldn't know of his involvement in the drama even if they had heard reports of what was happening in the sleepy little county town of Oakminster. The police hadn't told him much more than they had on the last occasion, mainly that the gang were still trying to negotiate a safe passage out of the building. He was, however, able to tell the police that he and the others were all safe in the storeroom and that the gang had been unable to break their way in.

'That presumably reduces the gang's bargaining power,' observed Ritchie when Luke reported the details of his conversation with the police.

'What do you mean?' demanded Jo, and there was a touch of hysteria in her voice.

'Well, they might be telling the police that they will start bumping us off one by one if their demands aren't met—don't forget they don't know we have a phone and have been able to tell the police that they can't get at us.'

'Do you think they would have…done that?' Jo obviously couldn't put the awful possibilities into words. 'If they could have got at us, I mean…'

'Oh, I don't doubt it,' said Ritchie. 'They're a desperate lot, don't forget, and let's face it—they don't have much to lose, do they? What ever happens now, they'll go down for a long stretch.'

Further speculation was put on hold as Aileen and Lizzie began distributing the last of the tea, coffee and biscuits. 'Make the most of it,' said Aileen. 'Next time it will be a mug of water and either half a biscuit or a couple of sweets.'

A sort of euphoria seemed to grip the group as they ate and drank, and then when every last drop and crumb was gone a kind of lethargy fell over everyone even before Luke advised them all to try to make themselves as comfortable as possible and to get some rest.

'I know it won't be easy,' he said as there were groans of protest. 'I know it's hot, I know you are all hungry and I know the floor is very hard, but it could be worse.'

'How much worse?' said Lizzie with a short scornful laugh.

'Much, much worse,' replied Luke firmly. 'It could be cold, we could all be suffering from hypothermia. We could have no toilet facilities and we could have no water.'

'And worse than all of that,' said Ritchie, 'there might not have been those filing cabinets in here, in which case we wouldn't now be thinking about how hot or cold or uncomfortable we are because we probably wouldn't be around to tell the tale.'

There was silence after that and Luke eased himself down to sit on the floor beside Ellie, their backs against the wall, where they could keep an eye on Denise, her baby and Brian.

After a time he boldly reached out and took Ellie's hand, encircling it with his own and squeezing it tightly for a moment. She didn't withdraw her hand. On the contrary, surprisingly, her own grip tightened fractionally, which gave him all the encouragement he needed not to release her. 'Are you all right?' he murmured softly at last, so softly that only Ellie could hear him.

She inhaled deeply, her nostrils flaring, and he had to fight a sudden urge to lean forward and cover her mouth with his own. 'Yes,' she said at last, oblivious to his almost uncontrollable desires, 'I think so...'

'You're worried, aren't you?'

'Worried...?'

'About your own baby.' There, he'd said it.

Her eyes widened slightly. 'My baby...?'

'I do know, Ellie,' he said softly.

'You know...?' she stared at him, her grip tightening on his hand.

'Yes,' he said. 'Reece told me, and I couldn't help overhearing you just now when you were talking to your mother. Jamie, that's his name, isn't it?'

'Yes, Luke, it is. But...but you need to understand something... After you went away—'

'Ellie,' he interrupted her quickly, 'I'm not blaming you...really I'm not. Please, don't think that. We had effectively ended our relationship before I went to the States.'

'I know but maybe I should have—'

'I couldn't expect you to have waited around on the off chance that I might come back.' He carried on talking, silencing whatever she had been about to say.

'No, that's true,' she agreed. 'Even so, maybe I should have—'

'It was inevitable that you should have found someone else,' he went on. It had to be said. The air between them had to be cleared if they were to move on and hopefully establish some new relationship.

'Someone else?' she said weakly.

'Yes, a beautiful woman like you—there was no

way you were going to be on your own for long, and
after all four years is a long time. That's not to say
that I don't get a surge of jealousy every time I think
of you with this other guy, but I can't help it. I guess
that's just me and I guess I've only got myself to
blame.'

There was silence for a long moment and he threw
a sideways glance at Ellie's profile—the short straight
nose, the way her lashes brushed her cheek, the curve
of her upper lip and the soft luscious fullness of her
lower lip—and once again the fight against desire was
on.

'Luke.' Ellie spoke at last, her voice barely more
than a whisper. 'There's something I need to tell
you—'

'Not now.' Reaching out his other hand, he touched
her lips with his finger, which did nothing to quell
the fire of passion deep inside that was threatening to
flare right out of control. 'I don't think I could bear
hearing any details about this other guy right now.'

'But—'

'No, Ellie, not now. It'll keep. Let's just get out of
here safely first. There will be plenty of time after
that to fill in any relevant details of the past few
years.'

Ellie seemed to slump a little at his words then after
a while he felt her rest her head against his shoulder,
and when at last he dared to glance down it was to
find that her eyes were closed. Carefully, so as not to
disturb her, he rested his head back against the wall
and somewhat surprisingly felt his own eyelids begin
to grow heavy.

Images flooded his mind, images of Ellie and the
way she had once filled his senses and his very life,

of how she had looked the first time he had seen her, in her white coat, with her hair drawn severely back and wearing her reading glasses. There had been something very sexy about that. He suddenly realised that since he'd been back he hadn't seen her wearing glasses. Maybe she now wore contact lenses, he would have to ask her. It was just one of the things he no longer knew about her, there must be countless others.

So much could have and had happened in those four years since he'd been away. She was now a mother, for one thing, and although her figure was still slender there was a slight voluptuousness that maybe hadn't been apparent before, a fullness to her breasts, a rounding of her hips and stomach. Such thoughts were dangerous and inevitably led him to recall that first time they had made love. They had been to a party, the wine had flowed and they had danced together in a small, very confined space. Then she had gone back with him to the rooms he had been renting in a large old house owned by the hospital as accommodation for their staff. They had been seeing each other for several weeks and Luke had wanted her from the moment he'd set eyes on her. She had seemed rather more restrained and he'd had to over-come his frustration until that night of the party, when any inhibitions she'd had had seemed to be discarded.

Maybe it had been the wine, he didn't know, but he certainly hadn't argued about it when she'd agreed to go home with him. And when at last he'd made love to her it had been everything he had hoped for, and, if her unexpected passion had been anything to go by, the experience had been equally delightful for her. It had been quick that first time, he remembered ruefully, because he'd been totally overcome. But later, when he'd had time to recover, he had reached out for her again, thrilled that her eagerness had matched his own, and this time he had been able to slow the pace as every desire for each of them was fulfilled, their love-making lasting throughout the night.

And they were together again, in these most bizarre of circumstances. While he had done his best to re-assure Ellie and some of the others that the immediate danger from the gang was over, he knew he couldn't be one hundred per cent sure of that. There was always the awful possibility that the bank robbers might be able to force their way into them or maybe even— perish the thought—start a fire or smoke them out. The list of possibilities was endless and if any of these things materialised, the threat of the hostage situation would still exist. He knew he shouldn't let his mind dwell on such things. The only way to get through this ordeal was to live one minute at a time and face each crisis as it occurred, instead of wasting energy on pointless speculation over what could happen. But that was easier said than done and he had to force himself to focus on other matters.

He found himself wondering about the youth, Ross, who had been shot, and whether the tourniquet he had applied was still effective or if the bleeding had started up again. He wondered about his parents on holiday in New Zealand and hoped they hadn't heard about the events in Oakminster. Once again, his thoughts turned to Ellie and his mind began to wander…

There was bright sunlight, blue, blue sky and miles of turquoise sea, white sandy beaches, waving palm trees, the cries of seabirds, shoals of tropical fish in crystal-clear waters…and Ellie. Ellie, who was beside him, above him, beneath him, who filled his senses, the taste of her, the scent, the feel of her…the sound of her laughter…

'Doc!' He came to with a start, opened his eyes and found Ritchie gently shaking his arm. It was dark in the storeroom except for a light from one of the toilets that someone had left on.

'What is it?' he asked urgently, instantly wide awake.

'It's him.' Ritchie pointed to Brian, who was muttering and moving his head from side to side.

Carefully, so as not to disturb Ellie, Luke crawled across the floor to the side of the injured man, placed one hand on his forehead and with the other took Brian's wrist and found a pulse.

'What is it?' said Ritchie anxiously.

'He's running a temperature,' said Luke, 'and he's delirious.'

'Can we do anything?' asked Ritchie.

'We can try and cool him down,' Luke replied. 'Could you fill the bowl in the kitchen with cold water and bring it in here with a teatowel if there are any left?'

Without a word Ritchie crawled away, clambering over others who had found themselves a small area of floor space, and a moment later Luke heard the sound of running water and low voices. Then Ritchie was back with the bowl of cold water and a piece of fabric, which he soaked in the water and lightly wrung out before passing it to Luke.

'Teatowel?' said Luke.

'No, Spencer's shirt,' Ritchie replied.

Luke gave a little grunt then proceeded to sponge the injured man's face and neck and the area of his chest that wasn't covered by the makeshift dressing that covered his wound. He kept this up for around ten minutes then he sat back on his heels. 'He's a bit cooler now,' he muttered at last.

'D'you think he's going to make it?' asked Ritchie doubtfully.

'I don't know,' Luke replied truthfully. 'He should have been in hospital hours ago.'

'Makes me wonder if any of us are going to make it,' said Ritchie gloomily.

'Don't let the ladies hear you say that,' murmured Luke.

'No, I know…but it does make you wonder.' Ritchie paused. 'It makes you think, too, doesn't it, Doc?'

'What do you mean?' Luke threw him a sidelong glance.

'Well, all this…the fact that we might all be staring death in the face. This morning I hadn't a care in the world—apart from my weight,' he added hastily, 'and in the space of a few hours I've had all sorts of thoughts going through my head. You know what I mean—things I wish I'd done and things I wish I hadn't. Truth is, Doc, my missus and me haven't been getting along too well recently and it's taken this to make me realise it's more my fault than hers. I've been playing away from home, you see. Don't know why I do it really—just because I can, I suppose.' He shrugged. 'But I wish I hadn't now.'

'Well, when we get out of here you can start making it up to her, along with this new lifestyle you're going to adopt,' said Luke philosophically.

'Yes, Doc, I reckon you're right,' said Ritchie with a sigh. 'That's all supposing we do get out, of course.'

'We will,' said Luke with more certainty than he was feeling.

At that moment the baby woke up and the sound of his cries filled the air and roused those who had drifted off to sleep. As Ellie opened her eyes Luke smiled at her.

'Hi, there,' he said softly. It was what he used to say when they'd spent the night together and she'd first opened her eyes and now, by the expression in her eyes, for the merest fraction of a second, before memory returned, it was as if that was what had just happened—that they had made love and spent the night in each other's arms and she had woken up to find him there beside her instead of in the dire situation which was reality.

CHAPTER EIGHT

WHEN Ellie opened her eyes and found Luke there and when he said, 'Hi there,' just in the way he used to do when they had been together, for one fleeting moment she thought that was how things were, that she and Luke were one, just like they had once been. And then, even as she still gazed at his dear face, unable to see the expression in those tawny eyes in the half-light, memories began filtering through the mist that surrounded her brain. She was no longer with Luke; he had gone away; Jamie had been born; then Luke had come back…and now…now… Wildly she looked around her as her brain finally clicked into gear and she remembered the events of the past hours and where she was. A thin wailing sound could be heard and just for one moment she thought it was Jamie then immediately she remembered that Denise had had her baby and it was that baby, Sam, whose cries now filled the air.

'I must go and help Denise,' she muttered, rubbing her eyes in disbelief that she had actually managed to sleep.

'She's all right,' said Luke reassuringly.

'Is everyone else OK?' Ellie glanced around.

'Brian has a fever,' Luke replied.

'I thought that might happen,' Ellie replied. 'Can we do anything?'

'Ritchie got some cold water and between us we

managed to sponge him down. He's a little quieter now.'

'You should have woken me up,' said Ellie. 'I can't believe I actually slept.'

'Exhaustion took over,' said Luke, 'which, I guess, is what happened with some of the others.'

'What's the time?' Ellie moved then groaned at the stiffness of her legs.

Luke peered at the luminous dial of his watch. 'It's just after four-thirty,' he said, then glanced up at the small skylight. 'It'll be light soon,' he added.

'Has there been any noise from outside?'

Luke shook his head. 'No, nothing.'

'Maybe they've been asleep as well,' said Ellie weakly as she scrambled to her feet and stretched.

'Somehow I doubt it,' said Luke grimly.

Ellie made her way across to Denise, who was sitting with her back to the wall, her baby in her arms. She lifted her head as Ellie approached.

'How are you feeling, Denise?' she asked.

'Stiff and very sore,' said Denise, 'and I can't stop him crying…' Helplessly she looked down at the baby.

'I think we'll try putting him to the breast,' said Ellie as she knelt down beside Denise.

'But there won't be any milk there yet,' Denise protested.

'Maybe not,' Ellie replied, 'but you will be producing colostrums, which is very nourishing. Let's give him a try and afterwards we'll get you both cleaned up as best we can.' Within moments baby Sam was suckling happily.

'There you are, you see.' Gently Ellie cupped the

baby's head in her hand and gazed down at him. 'That was all he wanted.'

As she watched the baby she inevitably found her thoughts drifting to Jamie and of how he had been at this stage when he had been less than a day old. Her circumstances had been vastly different from Denise's, of course, the only real similarity being that in neither case had the baby's father been present. Uneasily her gaze flickered across the room to Luke, who was tending to Brian. Earlier, when she'd realised that Luke knew she had a child she had almost confessed all, had been on the point of telling him that Jamie was his. But for some reason he had stopped her, saying there would be time for explanations later. He had talked as if he believed that her child was the result of another relationship, one she'd had after he had left. Could she, should she go on letting him believe that? The events of the last day had shaken her so much that she knew deep down in her heart that she should tell Luke that he was a father. Whether or not she would still feel that way when, or if, they ever got out of this place, she really didn't know. She would simply have to wait and see.

Gradually the others began to move, and those who had managed to snatch a couple of hours sleep woke up. People took turns for the toilets, and in the kitchen the remains of a bottle of squash was divided amongst everyone, together with the packet of mints.

'I hope this isn't going on for much longer.' Aileen spoke for them all. 'I never knew I could feel so hungry.'

'It could get worse before it gets better,' said Ritchie dully.

'What are the police doing? That's what I want to

know,' said Pauline helplessly. 'Why can't they just break down the doors and overpower that lot out there?'

'They have to be careful.' Luke spoke as if he detected a rising note of panic again amongst the others. 'Whatever they do will be criticised. They need to conduct this operation with the least possible number of casualties.'

'Well, if they don't hurry up, they'll have a roomful of casualties,' said Spencer, 'because we'll all have starved to death.'

'It takes longer than a day to starve, young man,' observed Violet, 'much longer, believe me. And because we have water, it'll take longer still.'

'I want to go home.' Jo began to cry and Lizzie put her arm round her in an attempt to comfort her. 'I want my mum…'

Somehow over the next hour Luke and Ritchie managed to sponge Brian down again and give him water to drink while Ellie, with Pauline's help, managed to wash both Denise and the baby and afterwards to wrap the baby in Denise's blouse, which she willingly discarded.

'Do you have children?' Ellie asked Pauline as they washed out the soiled teatowels that had previously been used on the baby.

'Yes.' Pauline nodded. 'I have three—two boys and a girl. Actually, I'm worried sick about my eldest son—he's on his gap year, you see, before going to university. He's been backpacking in Australia and South-East Asia and just before this happened we hadn't heard from him for a few days. We were just starting to worry—we always heard every two days or so.'

'Maybe your husband will have heard in the meantime,' said Ellie hopefully.

'He hadn't when I phoned him on Violet's phone,' Pauline replied, biting her lip as she struggled to control her emotions.

It was about an hour later, just before six o'clock, when the sun had climbed sufficiently high to shine through the narrow skylight, that they heard the first noises from outside. Everyone immediately grew still and listened, but the noises seemed to be coming from a long way off.

'Do you think…?' whispered Jo.

'Shh,' said three others in unison.

There was silence for a further agonising ten minutes during which, no doubt, many prayers were sent heavenwards, then came the sounds they had all been waiting for—persistent knocking on the storeroom door and a voice informing those inside of the presence of the police and instructing someone to open the door.

'Oh, thank God,' sobbed Jo.

'At last,' breathed Denise, holding her baby a little tighter.

But even as Ritchie and Spencer moved forward to move the filing cabinets in order for the police to gain access, Luke stopped them. 'Wait!' he ordered.

'Why?' demanded Jo hysterically. 'What's wrong now?'

'We have to be certain it really is the police,' Luke replied calmly.

The others stared at him. 'You mean…' Ritchie's eyes narrowed. 'You think it could be them trying to trick us into opening the door?'

'You mean, to take us as hostages again?' Spencer's face crumpled at the prospect.

'It's a possibility,' said Luke.

The shouting in the corridor was still going on and the knocking on the door grew louder. Ellie wasn't sure what was louder—the hammering on the door or the beating of her own heart. All she knew was that she wanted the whole thing to be over so that she could hold Jamie in her arms again, but at the same time she could see the sense of what Luke was saying. They had to be sure that it was the police who were outside, because if it wasn't and the thugs gained access to them again, she didn't know what would happen.

'Luke.' Urgently she tugged at the sleeve of his jacket. 'How can we be sure it's the police?'

'That's simple,' he replied in the same calm tones. 'I phone them before we open the door.' He paused and looked towards the kitchen. 'Violet,' he called, 'your phone, please, just one more time.'

Violet appeared in the doorway, her wrinkled face grim but purposeful, her white hair awry as she handed over the tiny instrument that had been their lifeline. Luke dialled the emergency number and everyone waited, hardly daring to breathe as he was put through to someone who would deal with his call. Eventually they heard him pose the crucial question then they saw him lower his head and briefly close his eyes.

'Luke…?' said Ellie.

He lifted his head. 'Come on, Ritchie, Spencer,' he said, 'let's move those cabinets.'

A cheer went up from the others, second only in volume to the one when Sam had been born, and

within seconds Luke, Spencer and Ritchie were eas-
ing the heavy cabinets away from the door.

The next hour was as much a blur to Ellie as the
raid itself had been because everything happened so
fast. In no time at all the room was full of police
officers, some in uniform, and others in plain clothes.
There might have been a stampede amongst those
who had been held captive for so long but one police
officer took charge. 'I'm Chief Inspector Dickinson,'
he said, identifying himself. 'I'm in charge of this
operation. You have all been through a dreadful ordeal and I'm sure you can't wait to be reunited with
your families, but I have to ask you all to remain
exactly where you are just for the moment.'

'I want to go home,' sobbed Jo.

'Yes, young lady, I'm sure you do,' the chief inspector replied, 'but we need to deal with any injuries
first.' As he spoke three medical staff came into the
room.

'Dr Barron?' One of the men who introduced himself as a doctor from the local hospital immediately
recognised Luke and looked to him to update them
on the medical situation.

'First priority is this man.' Luke indicated the manager lying on the floor. 'His name is Brian Westwood,
he was shot when he tried to raise the alarm. The
wound was bleeding profusely at the time but, using
pressure, we managed to stem the bleeding. He has
drifted in and out of consciousness ever since but in
the last few hours his temperature has risen. We
sponged him down with cool water but that was all
we were able to do. Secondly, we have this lady...'
his gaze moved to Denise '...who gave birth last
night.'

'We were told you had a pregnant lady in here,' said the doctor. 'What we didn't realise was that she'd actually had the baby.'

The two paramedics who had accompanied the doctor swung into action and an intravenous drip was set up. Watched by his silent companions, Brian was taken out on a stretcher, presumably to a waiting ambulance. While this was happening a second team of paramedics came into the room to deal with Denise and baby Sam.

'It's getting awfully crowded in here,' said Aileen with a touch of wry humour.

Ellie crouched down beside Denise and took her hand. 'It's all over now, Denise,' she said softly. 'You'll soon be with your husband and Mollie.'

'I'll never be able to thank you enough,' whispered Denise, 'you and Doctor Barron.' She looked exhausted, her face white with dark purple smudges beneath her eyes. 'It could have all gone so terribly wrong.'

'But it didn't.' Gently Ellie touched the soft down on Sam's head. 'It all went right and we have this gorgeous little chap to prove it.' She looked up as the paramedics prepared to help Denise into a wheelchair to transport her to an ambulance.

'How did you cope?' asked one paramedic, a note of awe in her voice.

'We improvised,' Ellie replied. 'We used the laces from someone's trainers as clamps and cut the cord with nail scissors.'

'The placenta?'

'It was intact as far as I could see,' Ellie replied, 'but you'll find it wrapped in a teatowel in the washbasin in one of the toilets.'

'Good grief,' said the woman. 'This hasn't exactly been a picnic, has it?'

'You can say that again,' said Ellie grimly.

'What about the baby?'

'He seems absolutely fine. The birth was straight-forward, fortunately, and he appears to be a good weight. We've put him to the breast this morning. He's passing meconium and crying normally—all the things you would expect of a day-old baby.'

'And the mother?' The paramedic glanced down at Denise, who was being wheeled out of the room.

'She's OK.' Ellie nodded. 'Exhausted, of course, and very anxious, but OK.'

'Blood loss?'

'Normal.'

'Good. Right, well, we'll get them both straight into A and E so they can be checked over, but it looks to me as if you've done a fantastic job here.'

'Is there anyone else who is injured or ill?' asked the doctor, looking round at the silent ring of faces.

'I don't think so,' said Luke, but even as he spoke Ellie glanced at the others and saw that Ritchie was clutching his chest.

'Ritchie…?' She moved towards him. 'What is it?'

'Chest pain…' he gasped. 'Terrible pain…'

'Let's get this man onto some oxygen to help him breathe,' said Luke urgently.

'Oh, no,' whimpered Lizzie, 'not Ritchie. He's been so good to us all…'

They all watched in silence as Luke, the other doctor and the paramedics fought to stabilise Ritchie, After an injection of adrenalin and with an oxygen mask covering his face, he too was borne swiftly away.

'I think it was moving those heavy cabinets that did it,' muttered Spencer. 'I didn't think he looked too good at the time…'

'He'll hopefully be all right,' said Luke, 'once they get him to hospital.'

'Right, as for the rest of you.' The police officer looked round at the ring of white, exhausted faces. 'You, too, are to be taken to hospital to be checked over.'

'I'm all right…' Jo began to sob and shake again. 'I don't want to go to hospital. I want to go home…'

'Jo.' Ellie put her arm around the girl in an attempt to comfort her. 'You could be suffering from shock, we probably all are. It's best to do as they say, then you'll be able to go home.'

'All right…' Jo gulped and blew her nose.

'What happened?' Luke turned to the chief inspector. 'The gang, I mean. How did you get in?'

Silence fell again as they all waited for the officer's reply. 'A special team of officers forced entry just before six o'clock,' he said at last. 'We met no resistance,' he added, to the amazement of those listening.

'No resistance?' It was Aileen who put it into words. 'So what happened to them?'

'They gave in without a fight in the end,' the officer replied.

'Without a fight…?' spluttered Spencer. 'I don't believe it. They shot Mr Westwood—Brian—for pity's sake, and they may have been going to start shooting us one by one if their demands weren't met.'

'What happened to the lad who was with them,' said Luke quietly, 'the one who'd been shot?'

'He was in a pretty bad way,' the officer replied. 'We think that's why they gave in eventually.'

'Will he make it?' asked Luke.

'We don't know.' The officer shook his head. 'He's on his way to hospital now and the others are in custody.' He paused and looked around again. 'Now, let's be moving you all. I'm sure you're all in need of food and drink.'

'You can say that again,' muttered Pauline.

'Oh, just one thing,' said the officer as he turned to lead the way out of the room. 'Who had the mobile phone?'

'It was mine.' Violet stepped forward. 'They told me to give it up, but there was no way I was going to do that. It was a present, you see, from my grandson.'

'Right, love.' The officer stared at her in awe. 'Well, that was very brave of you. And I can tell you it was of great assistance to us to know just what was going on in here. But if it happens again, I would have to advise you to do what you are told, especially if the one telling you has a gun.'

There were a few weak chuckles as everyone trooped out of the room that had been their prison for eighteen traumatic hours.

All Ellie really wanted to do was to go home, home to her mother and Jamie, to fold Jamie into her arms and to hold him like she would never let him go. But as she'd told Jo, she appreciated the sense of going to hospital and being checked over. A strange silence hung over the group as they left the storeroom and walked in single file into the staff area of the bank. Everywhere was evidence of what had happened. Broken glass surrounded the desks and on the carpet an ominous dark red stain marked the spot where Brian had been shot and had later lain until he had been dragged into the storeroom. In the public area there were further signs of the chaos that had reigned earlier—upturned chairs, more broken glass, further bloodstains around the doors and smears across the floor, presumably where the gang member had been shot before the gang had barricaded themselves inside the bank when their mission had gone so disastrously wrong. And in the middle of the floor was a little heap of mobile phones.

'Can we have them back now?' asked Lizzie.

'No.' One of the uniformed officers who was accompanying them answered her question. 'Nothing is to be touched until Forensics have been in.'

Two ambulances were waiting to transport them and as they stepped outside a thin cheer went up from a group of curious well-wishers who had gathered in the high street.

Ellie took a deep breath as the fresh air hit her and in silent thankfulness she briefly lifted her face to the sun.

'Looks like we're famous,' said Aileen as she sat beside Ellie in the back of one of the vehicles. 'Look, those are television cameras over there, aren't they?'

'They certainly are,' replied the policewoman who was accompanying them. 'You've made the national and the international news.'

'Well, they say everyone has fifteen minutes of fame in a lifetime, don't they?' Aileen smiled weakly. 'I guess this is ours. It would have been nice to have had a chance to tidy up a bit first, though—I'll probably never be on the telly again and I must look like something the cat dragged in.'

Ellie glanced at Luke and saw lines of fatigue around his eyes, and suddenly, almost desperately she wanted to reach out and touch him. Only hours earlier he had taken her hand and held it, and she had rested her head on his shoulder and slept. It had maybe been a forced intimacy, arising from the situation they had found themselves in and fuelled by a sense of danger, but it had been there, it had happened and briefly it had been a return to the way things had once been between them.

Now the situation and the danger were over, so was the need for intimacy. Now they were back in the real world and presumably they would return to the way they had been prior to when they had entered the bank. During that time of uncertainty she had almost told him about Jamie, had seen the necessity for him to know that he had a son, but now that the urgency of that moment had passed, did she still feel inclined to tell him or was it easier to allow him to assume that she had indeed had a relationship with someone else after he had left?

Maybe that wasn't the thing to do, she thought as she studied the weary lines of his profile, but for the moment, as utter exhaustion began to steal over her, she knew it would have to suffice.

'I do hope my cat is all right.' Violet suddenly broke the silence that had descended on the five of them travelling in the back of the first vehicle—herself, Ellie, Luke, Aileen and Spencer.

'I'm sure he will be,' said Ellie automatically, her thoughts still on Jamie and Luke. 'At least you know he'll be pleased to see you.'

'Don't you believe it,' Violet replied briskly. 'He sulks if I leave him for too long and refuses to have anything to do with me.'

'He's lucky to have someone who cares about him

so much,' said Luke, and Ellie shot him a sidelong glance. Was he implying that he had no one to care for him? Before she could say anything he turned to Spencer. 'What about you, Spencer?' he said. 'Is there someone who will have worried themselves silly over you?'

'Well, my mum probably will have done…' He hesitated and threw a glance at Aileen then, as if reaching a decision, he said, 'And my partner, of course.'

'Your partner?' Aileen looked up and frowned. 'Didn't know you had a girlfriend, Spence. You've kept that one quiet.'

'Actually, it isn't a girl,' said Spencer quietly.

Aileen stared at him in astonishment. 'Not a girl…' she said stupidly, then as realisation dawned she said, 'I had no idea…none of us did…'

'Is it a problem?' Spencer glanced at Ellie and Luke and suddenly Ellie felt sorry for him in that he'd felt compelled to make this revelation about himself at such a time.

'No,' said Aileen hastily, 'no, of course not. It's just that we didn't know…'

They were silent for several minutes then Aileen spoke again. 'Were we so awful, Spencer,' she said, 'that you felt you couldn't tell us?'

He shook his head. 'No,' he said, 'of course not. It's just that I thought you might not understand…and I liked you all so much. I didn't want to lose your friendship…'

'Oh, Spencer…' Aileen shook her head and pressed one hand against her mouth.

'Well, young man,' said Violet, 'now you've got that out of the way you can get on with the rest of your life.' Turning to Luke, she carried on in the same tone, 'And what about our doctor here? I'm sure there must be someone at home waiting for your return.'

For some reason Ellie found she was holding her breath as she waited for his reply.

'No, not really,' he said easily at last. 'My parents are on holiday in New Zealand. Hopefully they won't have heard about any of this.'

'They said we'd reached the international news,' said Aileen quickly.

'True,' Luke agreed, 'but knowing my parents they'll be halfway up some mountain or fishing in the middle of a lake, well away from news bulletins.'

'And you're telling me there isn't anyone else?' Violet raised her eyebrows, her shrewd gaze summing up Luke.

'Not really.' He shrugged and carefully avoided looking at Ellie.

'Well, maybe there isn't anyone who doesn't already know,' Violet replied cryptically, her gaze flickering to Ellie.

Thankfully for Ellie, they reached the hospital at that moment and the vehicle carrying them came to a halt, leaving no time for further speculation.

CHAPTER NINE

FREEDOM had never tasted so sweet and as Luke helped Violet and then Ellie from the back of the ambulance and walked beside them into A and E he marvelled at the lucky escape they had all had. It could have all ended so differently.

The gang could have decided to sit it out, in which case hunger and lack of medical supplies would soon have started to become a major factor and in the end the police would have had no choice than to storm the building. This, Luke was convinced, would have ended in even more bloodshed and possible loss of life, if not for the little group incarcerated behind the storeroom door, then amongst the members of the gang and quite possibly the police or special forces.

He had been surprised to learn that the police had not met with any resistance and he wondered whether this had come about after dialogue between the gang and the police or whether the police had decided it was time to break in. The officer had indicated that it was because of the injured man, Ross, but no doubt they would hear more in due course. Luke wanted to know more about Ross and his condition but first, along with the others, he had to face being checked over by medical staff himself.

He was concerned about Ellie. While she'd shown no signs of distress in the storeroom, he'd noticed that she'd grown very quiet in the ambulance, and when he helped her to alight her hands were shaking.

'Are you all right?' he murmured, taking her arm.

'Yes.' She nodded. 'I'm fine.' But he'd suspected that, along with several of the others, she was suffering either from delayed shock or post-traumatic stress syndrome. In either case treatment would be required and with a sense of frustration that he could do nothing further, either for Ellie or for any of the others, Luke watched as she was borne away to a treatment room by a staff nurse.

When his own medical examination was over Luke took a shower. Standing in the jet of tepid water as it doused his head, his face and his entire body, it was as though the water could wash away not only the sweat and grime and the blood of others but also every trace of the ordeal he'd been through. Only when he stepped from the shower and dried himself, rubbing his body vigorously with a rough towel, did he realise quite how hungry he was.

A staffroom had been set aside for the victims of the bank raid and when Luke arrived following his shower, he found that food from the hospital kitchens had been delivered—bacon sandwiches and huge mugs of hot, sweet tea.

After a while Luke was joined by Spencer and Lizzie, who both pounced on the food and devoured it in silence.

'Well, thank heavens for that,' said Lizzie, at last sitting back in satisfaction. 'My stomach was beginning to think that my throat had been cut.'

'Is Jo all right?' Luke poured himself a second mug of tea.

'They said she is being treated for shock,' said Lizzie. 'And someone said they are bringing in some counsellors for anyone who needs counselling.'

'All I want is some sleep,' said Spencer with a yawn. 'Do you think we can go home now?'

'Not yet.' Luke shook his head then nodded towards a policeman who was standing outside in the corridor. 'Apparently we all have to give statements to the police before we can go.'

Lizzie groaned. 'That'll take hours,' she said, then looked up quickly as the door suddenly opened and Pauline came into the room, her hair still wet from the shower.

'Hi.' She looked around at the others. 'Is that bacon I can smell?'

Gradually the others arrived one by one, but by the time Luke was called to give his statement to the police, Ellie still hadn't arrived and even later, when transport was made available to start taking some of the group home, he still hadn't seen her. In the end he could bear it no longer and asked the sister in charge of A and E if Ellie was all right.

'She's fine,' he was told briskly, 'but she was suffering from shock and she's resting quietly.'

'Can I see her?' he asked.

'Well, I don't know…Dr Barron…really…'

'Please, Sister,' said Luke intently, looking directly into the woman's eyes.

'Oh, very well,' the sister relented, 'just for a moment, then.'

Ellie was resting on her side on a narrow hospital couch in a cubicle, her back to the curtains. Luke stood quietly for a long moment just looking at her, at the gentle curve of her body beneath a cellular blanket, the long strands of her hair against the whiteness of the pillow, and he was overcome by a sudden rush of emotion as his brain acknowledged the true calibre of the trauma they had both been through.

She turned her head then as if she sensed him standing there. 'Luke…?' she murmured. 'What is it?'

'Nothing,' he said. Moving forward, he took the hand she reached out to him, lacing his fingers with hers, then sat beside her on the bed. 'It's nothing, Ellie, there's nothing wrong,' he said quickly, reading the sudden flash of anxiety in her eyes. 'I just wanted to see that you are all right.'

'Yes,' she said, 'I'm fine. I must have fallen asleep. I didn't mean to…'

'Shock and exhaustion got the better of you,' he said simply.

'What's happening?' she asked, looking beyond Luke to the opening in the curtains. 'Can we go home yet?'

'We all have to give a statement to the police first. Oh, and there are bacon sandwiches if you want them.'

Ellie managed a weak smile and his heart suffused with sudden love for her, a love which made him want to protect her for all time, never letting harm come to her ever again.

And then the sister was there, telling him it was time to go and telling Ellie that her mother had phoned and was on her way to the hospital to collect her.

'I'd best get this statement done,' said Ellie, struggling to sit up. Turning to Luke, she said, 'How will you get home?'

'Don't worry about me,' said Luke. 'I'll be fine. I'll give you a ring tomorrow.'

And then, before he knew it, it was all over and he was being taken home in a police car. As the car drew away from the hospital entrance, he glanced back and saw Violet being taken to a car by a tall, studious-looking man—presumably her very relieved son—and at the same moment Ellie's mother, Barbara, hurrying up the steps into the building to collect her daughter.

'Mum…' Ellie felt her mother's arms go round her and for a moment she was content to rest there just as if she were a child again.

'Ellie, darling…' Barbara held Ellie tightly, her voice thick with emotion, her cheeks damp with tears. 'Thank God,' she murmured, at last holding Ellie away from her and gazing anxiously into her face. 'Thank God you are safe.' She swallowed as if trying desperately to get her emotions under control. 'You are all right, aren't you?' she added.

'Yes, Mum, I'm OK,' she said. 'Jamie…?' she added, looking around.

'He's fine,' said Barbara quickly. 'He's at nursery. I…I thought it best to keep things as normal as possible. He missed you last night, of course, then again this morning he kept asking for you, but when we heard on the news that you had all been released I thought it best to stick to his usual routine. I hope I did right.'

'Oh, Mum, of course you did.' Ellie laughed weakly. 'Honestly, one of the things that kept me going in there was the fact that I knew Jamie was safe with you.'

'And do you know the thing that kept me going?' said Barbara breathlessly. When Ellie shook her head, she went on, 'The fact that they said that Luke—Dr Barron—was in there with you.'

'I know.' Ellie lowered her head. 'Luke was a tower of strength to everyone.'

'I can imagine,' Barbara replied.

'He…he…quite simply took control,' said Ellie, her voice shaking. 'He even patched up one of the gang who'd been…shot.' Her voice cracked.

'Is he here?' Barbara looked around.

Ellie shook her head. 'No, he's just been taken home in a police car.'

'I could have taken him home,' said Barbara then added more briskly, 'But never mind, just as long as he's all right. The thing now is to get you home.'

'Oh, yes,' said Ellie softly. 'Yes, please.'

She was mostly silent on the drive to the cottage, mainly because she was assailed by a sense of disorientation and feelings of unreality—the fact that, in spite of all that she and the others had been through, outside everything appeared exactly the same as it had always done. It was another very warm day, just as the previous day had been, the sun was shining brightly and the people of Oakminster were going about their daily business. The route from the hospital out of town unavoidably took them past the bank, and Ellie gave an involuntary shudder as she caught sight of the police barriers around the building and the two police cars that stood outside.

'What I couldn't understand,' said Barbara, casting a sidelong glance at her daughter as she drove past the building, 'was how you and Luke both came to be in the bank. I first heard the news on local radio and I didn't for one moment imagine that you were in any way involved, then the surgery phoned me to ask if you were at home. I told them you weren't and it was after that call that I began to suspect that you might have been inside the bank when the raid took place. William Stafford rang me back later to confirm it then, of course, you managed to phone. But I still wondered about you and Luke...'

'We went out to lunch together,' said Ellie. Had that only been yesterday? It seemed days ago now. 'We were walking back to the surgery and I needed to go to the bank. Luke came inside to wait for me— it was as simple as that.'

'And that's when...it happened...?'

'Yes,' Ellie gulped, and looked out of the car window through a sudden mist of tears. 'I'm sorry...I can't talk about it yet. I will later but not now. I need to see Jamie first.'

'Of course,' said Barbara. 'We'll get you home first then it'll be nearly time for me to go and collect Jamie.'

They drove the rest of the way in silence. When they reached the cottage Barbara made tea then Ellie took a bath before falling asleep on the sofa.

When she woke up she felt much better. The fog in her brain seemed to have cleared and she felt more in control of her thoughts and actions. The cottage was silent and she found a note from her mother saying that she'd gone to collect Jamie. As she read it she heard the slam of a car door then the excited, high-pitched chatter of a child. Looping her hair back behind her ears, she hurried to the door and flung it open. Jamie, laden with drawings and a cardboard cut-out of a tiger, was halfway up the path. His hair was tousled, his face flushed with anticipation, his eyes, so like his father's, alight with excitement. He stopped when he caught sight of Ellie then as she opened her arms he ran forward and she scooped him up, holding him as if she would never ever let him go.

'Jamie. Oh, Jamie.' She kissed him then nuzzled his neck.

'You didn't read story,' he said accusingly, squirming in her arms.

'No,' she admitted, half laughing, half crying, 'I didn't, did I? Tell you what, we'll have two stories tonight.' That satisfied Jamie and when he finally managed to disentangle himself from Ellie's grasp he trotted off to the kitchen for his customary orange juice and biscuit.

Later, much later, after Jamie had had his tea and she'd bathed him and put him to bed and had told him the promised two stories, she came downstairs and found her mother preparing a meal for them both.

'Is he all right?' asked Barbara, looking up from chopping vegetables.

'Yes, he's almost asleep,' Ellie replied.

'It's a good job he's too young to understand what was happening,' observed Barbara.

'That's true.' Ellie nodded. 'How soon will dinner be, Mum?' she asked after a moment.

'Oh, at least an hour,' Barbara replied. 'Why, was there something you wanted to do?'

'I need to phone someone from the surgery,' Ellie replied.

'Won't it be closed now?' Barbara glanced at the kitchen clock.

'Yes, but I'll phone William at home.' Leaving her mother in the kitchen, Ellie went into the sitting room to make her call. She still felt strange, as if every action she made was more deliberate and every image was somehow heightened. William answered the phone on the third ring and after he'd expressed his pleasure and relief at speaking to her, he went on to tell her not to think of rushing back to work.

'I've spoken to Luke,' he said, 'and he's given me an update on all that happened. He also told me that you are suffering from shock.'

'I feel a bit of a wimp,' she said. 'I am a doctor, for heaven's sake.'

'And you think that makes you immune to normal human reactions?'

'Well, no, I suppose not,' she said weakly.

'You've been through a traumatic experience,' he said. 'Just give yourself time to get over it. I've told Luke the same—to give himself a bit of space before coming back to work.'

'But how will you manage?'

'That's our problem,' William replied cheerfully. 'But don't you worry, manage we will.'

Then as she was about to hang up, a sudden impulse prompted her to ask for Luke's home telephone number. Moments later Luke was answering her call. He sounded surprised but pleased to hear from her.

'Are you feeling better?' he asked, and she could hear the genuine concern in his voice.

'Yes,' she said, 'much better, thanks. How about you?'

'I've had a sleep and a meal—it's amazing how much better that can make you feel. I have to say though there's a strange sense of unreality about it all now.'

'I know exactly what you mean,' said Ellie with a

sudden stab of relief, 'and I'm glad to hear you say it. I was beginning to think it was just me.'

'No, not at all,' Luke replied firmly. 'I guess we've just got to give ourselves a bit of time to get over it. Let's face it, Ellie, it wasn't the usual run-of-the-mill thing—I mean, it's not every day we're called upon to do what we've had to do, is it?'

'No, I guess not,' she replied faintly. 'I was thinking that as doctors we should have been able to take it in our stride and, well, you did, but I…' She broke off.

'Ellie,' said Luke quietly, 'you did everything that was required of you. There are some people back there who will have every reason to be extremely grateful to you.'

'I wasn't prepared for the shock…'

'That was because you faced personal danger,' he said, 'and I have to say scenes keep recurring in my mind. I guess that's just part of being human…'

'That's what William said.'

'You've spoken to William?'

'Yes, a moment ago. He said not to hurry back to work. And it was he who gave me your number.'

'Ah, I see.' He was silent for a moment and Ellie found herself wishing she could see him. Suddenly the thing she wanted most in the world was to feel Luke's arms around her. 'When…when will you go back?' she said at last in an effort to pull herself together.

'In a day or so,' he said. 'But you must take your time—get plenty of sleep.'

'I wonder how the others are—Denise, Ritchie and Brian… And…and that boy…'

'I'm planning to go back to the hospital tomorrow,'

said Luke. 'I'll check everyone out then I'll give you a ring and let you know.'

'Thanks, Luke,' she said. 'I would appreciate that.'

'How is your little boy?'

She swallowed. 'Yes, he's fine…thanks to Mum…' She hesitated then said, 'Well, I'd better go now, Luke.'

'All right, Ellie,' he said. 'Take care of yourself. I'll see you soon.'

'Yes, Luke. Good bye.' She hung up and sat for a long moment staring at the phone, thinking of him at home on his own and wishing that she could be with him.

Later, over dinner, she found herself wanting to talk about what had happened while Barbara, recognising her need, let her do so. She told of the shock and horror of the actual raid; of the manager being shot, of everyone, staff and customers alike, being herded into the storeroom by the masked gunmen. She told of Violet's defiance and bravery, of Denise's dread that harm would come to her unborn baby, then she explained how they had pooled resources and rationed anything edible. She went on to tell how they had barricaded themselves into the storeroom and how they had kept the police informed of what they had done. She fell silent for a moment, reflecting on all that had happened. At last Barbara looked up and Ellie somehow sensed what she was going to say.

'Ellie…about Luke,' she said, confirming Ellie's suspicion.

'What about Luke?'

'Well, he and you…you said before all this the two of you were having lunch together?'

'Yes.' Ellie nodded, recalling eating the hot cheese scones, which now seemed part of another lifetime.

'I wondered…did you say anything?'

'About Jamie, you mean?'

'Yes, of course about Jamie.'

'No.' She shook her head. 'I didn't feel inclined to, not while we were having lunch,' she added.

'Oh,' said Barbara, 'I see.'

'Later I wanted to tell him,' Ellie went on after a moment. She was aware of her mother's look of sudden interest. 'I tried,' she added, 'when I thought we might not get out of there alive. I really wanted him to know that he had a son. Suddenly it seemed the most important thing in the world.'

'So what happened—did you tell him?'

Ellie shook her head. 'No,' she said. 'Like I said, I tried, I said I had something to tell him but he stopped me, he said not at that time, but later. He knows I have a child,' she added, as it suddenly occurred to her that her mother didn't know that.

'How does he know that?' Barbara frowned.

'Reece Davies at the surgery told him.'

'Don't you think he may suspect that Jamie is his?'

'No.' Ellie shook her head. 'He thinks I had a relationship with someone else after he left for the States.'

'Maybe it really is time now that he learnt the truth,' said Barbara.

'Yes.' Ellie nodded and, leaning her head back, briefly closed her eyes. 'I think you are right.'

CHAPTER TEN

LUKE drove out of the parking space alongside the auction rooms and automatically found himself glancing up at the Minster clock. The hands stood at ten o'clock. He felt so much better that morning that it seemed ridiculous that he wasn't going into work, but William had been adamant that he take some time off. 'Just give yourself some space, Luke,' he'd said when they'd spoken the previous day on the phone.

'But I feel fine,' Luke had protested.

'Even so,' William had persisted. 'You've been through an unusual and highly traumatic experience and I don't think it appropriate that you should be sitting here for hours on end, listening to people's symptoms and ailments. At least give yourself a twenty-four-hour break.'

There had been no arguing with that and he'd been obliged to take the senior partner's advice. The press had phoned him, both local and national, but he'd been warned by the police not to give any interviews until after charges had been brought against the members of the gang, including the injured man.

In the end he'd been surprised by just how much he had needed to rest, and it even crossed his mind that he may have suffered a small degree of delayed shock. He'd also been surprised, pleasantly so, by Ellie's call because it seemed that she had simply wanted to talk to him, and had gone to the lengths of asking William for his home number. But it was inevitable that the circumstances of the last couple of days should have drawn them closer together.

But…and he hesitated over even trying to put his thoughts into any semblance of order…it had seemed to him that at times it had been more than that, more than the closeness of two people thrown together in exceptional circumstances, albeit two people with shared history. No, there had been something else, he could have sworn it.

When she had clung to him during the raid and immediately afterwards, there had been fear, terror even, but hadn't there also been something extra—or was he simply deluding himself? And later she'd fallen asleep on his shoulder with an ease and familiarity that had caused his heart to pound, and when she'd woken up and first seen him there had been an acceptance of him being there even before there had been time for her consciousness to kick in, as if for Ellie it had been the most natural thing in the world for him to be the first person she'd seen on waking up.

And it had been once, he reminded himself ruefully as he drove through the town. At one time he had been the most important person in her world and she in his—could that ever be the same way again? His pulse quickened at the thought and the blood pounded in his ears.

It was different now. He had been out of her life for four years and during that time she'd borne another man's child. She had wanted to tell him about that during the time they'd been held captive, almost as if it had been imperative to her that he should know, but he'd stopped her. He wasn't sure why now—he only knew that at the time it hadn't seemed appropriate and, if he was honest, it hadn't really mattered when they had been staring possible death in the face.

Before that time he hadn't been entirely certain that he would have been able to take on another man's child and raise him as his own, but somehow, now, after all they'd been through, it seemed of little consequence and there was no doubt in his mind that he would be able to do so. After all, this was Ellie's baby they were talking about.

He would go and see her. Maybe later that day after his visit to the hospital, he would go and talk to her, tell her he still loved her, hadn't stopped loving her, and ask her if she thought they could have another try at their relationship.

The thought of what he would do cheered him and lifted his spirits and by the time he reached the hospital he was in a much more positive frame of mind.

Oakminster Hospital was a large, modern building on the outskirts of the town, surrounded by lawns and flower-beds lovingly tended by the hospital's league of friends. It was another warm day but without the bright sunshine of previous days. Instead, great banks of dark cloud were building on the horizon, giving an overcast, oppressive feeling that suggested a thunderstorm might be about to end the spell of hot weather.

Luke's first visit after parking his car was to the hospital's coronary care unit, where the charge nurse on duty immediately recognised him. 'Dr Barron,' he said, looking up from the central, monitor-covered desk, 'I can guess why you're here this morning.'

'I'm sure you can.' Luke smiled. 'So how is Ritchie?'

'He's doing all right,' the charge nurse said, then

referred to a set of notes. 'He will be going for an angiogram later today—obviously we'll know more after that—but for the time being he's fairly stable. Perhaps you'd like to see him?'

'Yes, I would, please,' Luke said, and followed the nurse to a side ward where Ritchie, his eyes closed, was lying in bed connected to a heart monitor with pads attached to his chest and with medication being administered through an infusion via a cannula in his right hand.

'Hello, Ritchie.' Luke sat down on a chair beside the bed.

Ritchie opened his eyes and when he saw that Luke was his visitor he managed a weak smile. 'Hi, Doc,' he said.

'How are you feeling?' asked Luke.

'Better than I did yesterday,' Ritchie admitted. 'You know something? I thought I was a gonner.'

'It'd take more than that—armed gunmen, a bank raid and being held hostage—to finish you off, Ritchie,' said Luke with a chuckle.

'You're right,' Ritchie agreed. 'It was those filing cabinets that did it. They were damn heavy.'

'Has your wife been in?' asked Luke after a moment.

'Yes,' Ritchie replied. 'She was here best part of the night. I persuaded her to go home and get some rest. I said I'm not going to die yet and, besides, they want to do this angio thing this morning.'

'That's right.' Luke nodded. 'Remember, I said I wanted you to see a cardiologist. An angiogram is probably what he would have requested. It enables us to see whether you have any blockages in your blood vessels.'

'And if I have?' Ritchie raised one eyebrow.

'Then we can decide on any further treatment, maybe angioplasty where a stent is put into a vein or artery to keep it open. But let's not worry about that yet. First things first.'

'OK,' Ritchie said. 'Have you heard how that manager chap is?' he asked after a moment.

'No.' Luke shook his head then he stood up. 'But I'm going to try and find out now.'

'It was a right do, wasn't it, Doc?' said Ritchie, and Luke knew exactly what he meant.

'Yes, Ritchie,' he said quietly, 'it was. But we've all got to try and put it behind us now and get on with our lives.'

'I know,' said Ritchie, and briefly closed his eyes. As Luke moved away he spoke. 'Doc?' he said, opening his eyes.

'Yes?' Luke paused and looked down at him again.

'I'm going to make it up to the missus,' he said.

'Good,' Luke replied. 'I'm glad to hear it.'

After Luke left Ritchie he went to the surgical unit and made enquiries about Brian Westwood, only to be told that he had been taken to Theatre that morning.

'We couldn't operate before,' the registrar told him. 'His temperature was far too high and his blood pressure too low. He's a bit more stable this morning so hopefully the operation to remove the gunshot pellets will be successful.'

'And what about the lad with the bullet in his thigh?' asked Luke.

'He's over there.' The registrar indicated a ward separate from the others, where two uniformed police officers stood guard outside the door. Through the glass partition another could be seen at the bedside.

'Do they think he's going to make a bid for freedom in his condition?' asked Luke wryly.

'I don't think they intend taking any chances,' the registrar replied as he led the way to the glass partition.

'So how is he?' said Luke, as he looked through the glass at the young man on the bed.

'He was in poor shape when he came in,' the registrar replied. 'He'd lost a tremendous amount of blood before someone applied a tourniquet. We operated and removed the bullet from his thigh and he was given several transfusions. I think he'll pull through all right now.'

As Luke watched, Ross lifted his head and looked towards the glass partition, his gaze briefly meeting Luke's, recognition registering briefly before he turned his head away.

'That tourniquet definitely saved his life,' said the registrar as he and Luke turned away. 'At least now he'll be able to stand trial. Rumour has it that his older brother was also in the gang.'

'I would go so far as to say that's more likely to be a certainty than a rumour,' said Luke.

Luke's next port of call was to the postnatal unit, where he found Denise and baby Sam with her husband and her little daughter, Mollie, surrounded by masses of flowers and dozens of congratulation cards.

'Luke!' Denise looked overjoyed to see him.

'Just doing a round of patients,' he said with a grin. 'But I can see I don't have any concerns here.'

'Is Ellie with you?' asked Denise eagerly.

'No.' Luke shook his head. 'We've persuaded her to rest for a while.'

'Of course,' Denise agreed. Turning to her husband, she said, 'Dave, this is Luke—Dr Barron—who was in there with us…'

Dave Tolley immediately sprang to his feet and shook Luke warmly by the hand. 'Very pleased to meet you,' he said. 'From what Denise tells me, we have a great deal to thank you for.'

'Well, if it's the birth of your son you're referring to,' said Luke, 'then it's my colleague, Dr Renshaw, you have to thank. She was the one who was playing midwife.'

'I'll have to see her another time,' said Dave, 'and thank her properly, but it sounds as if you had your hands full as well, what with bullet wounds and heart attacks.'

'All part of the service,' said Luke with another grin as he bent down to admire baby Sam, who was sleeping peacefully in a hospital cot.

'Are they all OK?' asked Denise anxiously.

'Yes, they're fine,' Luke replied.

'Ritchie?' Denise frowned.

'He's going to have some treatment. Brian Westwood is in Theatre and Ross is recovering from surgery.'

'Ross?' said Dave.

'He was one of the gang—the one who got shot,' Denise explained. 'They made Luke patch him up, didn't they, Luke?'

'Yes, they did,' Luke replied.

'I bet you didn't feel like doing that,' observed Dave.

'I'm a doctor,' Luke replied with a little shrug.

'Even so...' Dave trailed off as Mollie tugged at his sleeve to show him a toy lamb that someone had sent as a present for the baby.

'Was Ellie's little boy all right?' asked Denise as she fondly watched her daughter.

'Yes, I think so,' Luke replied. 'Luckily, at his age he wouldn't have known too much of what was going on.'

'You'd be surprised,' Denise replied. 'This young lady knows far more than we give her credit for.'

'Yes, but she's a bit older than Ellie's little boy.'

'No.' Denise shook her head. 'Actually, they are the same age. They are both three.'

Luke stared at her. 'Are you sure?' he said at last. 'I thought Ellie's child was much younger, still a baby.'

'Oh, no,' said Denise, and something in Luke's brain seemed to shift a gear, 'she told me herself that he was three years old.'

Luke sat in his car in the hospital car park, his hands resting on the steering-wheel as he stared with unseeing eyes at the lawns and flower-beds before him. Just for a moment there, back in the postnatal ward as he'd stood beside Denise's bed, the world, or at least his world, had seemed to stand still as the implication of what Denise had just told him had sunk into his brain.

Until that moment his understanding had been that Ellie's child was a baby, which, much as he may not have wanted to accept the fact, had meant that it had been conceived while he had been in the States. Now he had learnt that the baby was, in fact, a three-year-old, which put a whole new connotation on the situation: at the time of this child's conception he and Ellie had most certainly been together.

The possibility that Ellie's child could be his had hit him with a mixture of shock, excitement and disbelief.

Surely, he reasoned, as he sat there in the car, surely Ellie would have told him. Even if she hadn't known before he'd gone to the States, she would have contacted him to let him know news of such importance. Surely she wouldn't have kept that from him? And if she had, for some obscure reason, decided not to tell him then surely when they'd met up again, working at the same surgery, she would have told him?

Wouldn't she?

The other possibility, of course, was that she'd had another relationship while she'd still been with him or immediately after he'd left. The thought left him uncomfortable, unable to believe that either.

There was, he knew, only one way to learn the answers to his questions, one way to put paid to further speculation, and that was to go and see Ellie and ask her for himself.

Taking a deep breath, he took his hands from the steering-wheel, started the engine and slipped the car into gear.

Ellie had decided not to send Jamie to nursery school that morning, instead wanting to keep him close to her after the horrors of two days ago. She'd slept badly, waking every hour or so, imagining she was back in the claustrophobic confines of the storeroom. And when she had slept she'd dreamt of shootings, of blood, of people dying, and once, terrifyingly, she'd dreamt that Jamie was missing and she wasn't able to find him. Luke had been there in her dreams, but for some reason he had always been just out of reach, an elusive, shadowy figure always on the edge of her line of vision and disappearing if she tried to touch him.

At last, just as dawn had been approaching, she'd fallen into a deep, dreamless sleep and when she woke up she felt tired and unrefreshed. A shower helped to revive her then she joined her mother in the kitchen where Jamie was already up and munching his way through a bowl of cereal.

'Hello, darling.' Barbara looked up as Ellie entered the room. 'Did you sleep well?'

'Not really.' Ellie shook her head. 'Too many demons in my brain.' She bent over and kissed the top of Jamie's head. He smelt of baby soap and orange juice. 'I've decided not to send him to nursery today,' she said.

'Oh?' Barbara looked up. 'I do need to get on with some work this morning,' she said. 'The art editor keeps ringing me…'

'It's all right,' Ellie replied quickly. 'I'll be here but I just want Jamie with me today. I thought I'd take him across to the green later to play football.'

'Football?' Jamie looked up, his eyes shining.

'Yes, darling,' said Ellie. 'You'd like that, wouldn't you?'

The little boy nodded then happily went back to his breakfast.

'There's quite a lot in the papers today about the bank raid,' said Barbara.

'Let me see.' Ellie leaned across the kitchen table and saw that the raid had made front-page news.

There was a large picture of Ritchie Austin, who was described as a wealthy, successful businessman, and one of bank manager Brian Westwood, who was being hailed as a hero and whose life was 'hanging in the balance' following the gunshot wounds he'd received in the raid. There was a picture of Luke taken when he and Ellie had worked at the same hospital and, surprisingly, one of Ellie herself at a party at the hospital.

'Where on earth did they get these?' she said incredulously. 'They must have been taken at least four or even five years ago.'

Someone must have spoken to the press in spite of being instructed not to because there was a report of Denise giving birth to her second child and the fact that the group had had contact with the outside world by a mobile phone belonging to an elderly lady.

'This will be all the patients will want to talk about when I get back to work,' said Ellie with a sigh as she closed the newspaper and poured herself a mug of coffee.

'It'll be a nine-day wonder,' Barbara remarked, 'then it will be on to something or someone else. I'm just thankful to have you back in one piece and for the fact that no one lost their lives.' She paused. 'Well, I suppose I'd better get on. Watch the weather if you're going out, won't you? It looks like we could be in for a storm.'

'Don't worry, I won't be going far,' Ellie replied.

Barbara took herself off to work to her little studio and after Ellie had tidied the kitchen and completed a few household chores she told Jamie to fetch his football. Hand in hand the two of them made their way across the road from the cottage to the village green. Within no time they were happily engaged in a game of football, or at least Jamie would kick the ball as far as he could then shriek with delight while Ellie ran after it.

Maybe because she was so happy to be enjoying time with her son, precious time which only hours before she had despaired she might never know again, Ellie failed to notice the black car that slid to a halt beside the green or its driver, who sat for some considerable length of time simply watching them play.

The first she knew of its presence was the sound of a car door being shut. As she glanced over her shoulder, the tall figure who climbed over the chain that linked the posts surrounding the green walked towards them across the grass.

As she realised it was Luke, her heart missed a beat and she automatically threw a frantic glance in Jamie's direction. She found herself holding her breath as Luke reached her, but instead of stopping he carried on walking until he reached the football, which he kicked back to the little boy.

Delighted that someone else had joined their play, Jamie kicked the ball back and Luke returned it. This went on for some minutes while Ellie, who felt her knees might be about to give way, sank down onto one of the wooden seats that surrounded the green and watched the two of them at play.

It was still hot and very oppressive and in the distance Ellie thought she heard the first far-off rumblings of thunder. Nervously she wiped her hands down the sides of her jeans. Although she had already decided that Luke would have to know about Jamie, she hadn't visualised it happening like this. She had imagined that she would tell him when they were on their own somewhere, perhaps over a meal where she could break the news gently. No doubt now he would have put two and two together.

After a while Jamie lost interest in the football and took himself off to the base of the oak tree, where he must have remembered the family of woodlice who had been there the last time they had visited the green, leaving Luke to pick up the ball then join Ellie on the seat.

They were silent for a while as they watched the little boy before them, and Ellie struggled to find the right words.

'Why did you come?' she said at last, unable to launch right in with the more difficult subject of Jamie's paternity.

'I went to the hospital,' he said, his gaze still on the child as if he were unable to tear it away.

'How were they…all of them?' she asked weakly.

'All right.' He nodded. 'Ritchie's having an angiogram today. Brian Westwood was in Theatre and Ross, well, he appears to be holding his own.'

'And Denise, did you see her?' Ellie turned her head to look at him but he was still watching Jamie.

'Yes,' he said, adding after a long pause, 'It was because of Denise that I'm here.'

'Oh?' Ellie frowned but she had an inkling of what he was going to say.

'She asked about you, Ellie, and about your little boy. I made a comment about him being too young to understand anything of what had gone on and she said that it was surprising how much a three-year-old was able to pick up. I told her that your child was still a baby, but she said, no, you had told her yourself that your little boy was three years old.' His eyes narrowed as he stared at Jamie. 'It seems she was right.'

Ellie remained silent, unable to find the right words to say, and after another long pause Luke spoke again. 'He's mine, isn't he?' he said, his eyes still on Jamie.

Ellie took a deep breath, vaguely aware that the threatening thunder was growing closer. 'Yes, Luke,' she said at last, 'yes, he is.'

He released his breath in a long drawn-out sigh.

'Why didn't you tell me?' he said at last, and his voice sounded husky with emotion, not like Luke's voice at all.

'I...I was going to.' Helplessly Ellie spread her hands.

Slowly Luke turned his head to look at her and just for a moment she was confused, frightened even by the look on his face—a look she'd never seen before. 'You were going to...?' he repeated.

'Yes...I...'

'When were you going to tell me?' His voice was low, intense with an edge of something that quite easily could have been anger. 'When he was five? Ten? Or maybe on his eighteenth birthday?'

'Luke, don't,' Ellie protested. 'Please, don't take it like that.'

'How did you expect me to take it?' He paused again, and when she shrugged he said, 'Why didn't you tell me, Ellie?' His voice was calmer now but it still had a raw, unfamiliar edge to it.

'You weren't here.' She shook her head, knowing it sounded weak.

'You mean you didn't know until after I'd gone?' He sounded faintly incredulous.

'I found out after we'd ended our relationship.'

'I can hardly believe it.'

'Well, I can assure you it's true.' There was an edge to her voice now. 'There wasn't anyone else,' she added, 'not then, or since.'

'I wasn't suggesting—'

'Unlike you,' she went on, not giving him chance to speak, 'who replaced me even before you'd left the country.'

'Replaced you?' He stared at her. 'Oh,' he said at last as enlightenment dawned. 'I suppose you're referring to Susie again. Well, I told you before, that was nothing. I'd had too much to drink—'

'Yes, I know, you said.'

'Surely it wasn't just because of that incident with Susie that you chose not to tell me that you were pregnant?' He sounded incredulous again.

'No,' she said quickly, 'of course not.'

'So why, then?'

'We had already parted, Luke. We had ended our relationship, you were going to the States and, well, it seemed for the best. You didn't want that sort of commitment—you said so.'

'And you agreed,' he said quickly.

'Because it was pretty obvious that was what you wanted,' she retorted hotly. 'You were career-building, Luke, and there was no room for long-term relationships or anything that remotely resembled that.'

'But you were pregnant, for God's sake. Do you not think I would have faced up to that—accepted my responsibilities?' He sounded shocked now, so shocked that Ellie felt the first pangs of doubt over the decision she had made to keep silent. But how could she tell him that she had never doubted that he would have taken responsibility for his child but that deep down she hadn't wanted that, had wanted him to want her for herself and not just because she had been carrying his child?

'Is that what you thought, Ellie?' he said, turning his head again to face her.

'No... I don't know...' She shook her head. 'I don't know what I thought, Luke. You had gone, I was pregnant, I just had to get on with things, it was as simple as that.' As she spoke the first drops of rain began to fall, great drops that plopped onto the grass, spattering onto the leaves of the oak trees above them.

'Raining, Mummy.' Jamie trotted back to Ellie and looked up into her face.

'Yes, darling,' she said at last, as they both stared at the little boy.

'Wet,' he said in delight as he lifted his face to the sky.

'I must get him home,' she muttered, rising to her feet. Looking down at Luke as he still sat there,' she said, 'Do you want to come back with us, Luke?'

'No.' He shook his head. 'I need some time, Ellie, some time to get my head around this.'

'Yes.' She nodded, then as the heavens opened she scooped Jamie up under her arm and ran across the green to the cottage. She looked back once and saw that Luke had remained where he was sitting on the bench in the pouring rain.

CHAPTER ELEVEN

'So how did he take it?'

'He was angry.'

'I'm not surprised, Ellie. I always thought he should have known.'

'Yes, I know you did,' Ellie sighed, 'but there's nothing I can do about that now.' It was later that day. Ellie had given Jamie his lunch and the little boy had gone for his nap and Barbara had joined Ellie for a quick lunch before returning to her work. Outside torrential rain was still falling, soaking into the dry parched earth of the cottage garden and rushing down the stone steps to the courtyard.

'So how did he find out? Did he see Jamie and just guess?' asked Barbara curiously as she bit into a sandwich.

'No, he'd been to the hospital,' Ellie replied, then went on to explain to her mother about Luke's conversation with Denise, which had prompted him to come to find her. 'But I think once he'd set eyes on Jamie it simply confirmed what she had told him.'

'But he was angry, you say?' Barbara frowned.

Ellie nodded. 'Yes, he couldn't understand why I hadn't told him.'

'Actually, darling, neither can I...'

'You know why,' Ellie retorted. 'Like I told Luke, our relationship was over by the time I found out I was pregnant and he went to the States almost im-

mediately. As far as I knew, he might never have
come back here.'

'But he did,' said Barbara gently. 'And even if he
accepts your reasons for not telling him then, I'm sure
he can't understand why you haven't told him since
his return.'

'I nearly told him…I told you that…'

'Yes, when you were in that awful place, but I
think that was a purely emotional response to the situation, and in the end you didn't tell him, did you?'

'No, I didn't,' Ellie replied quickly, 'but that was
only because he stopped me. He thought I was going
to explain that Jamie was the result of another relationship. I guess he didn't want to hear about that, at
least not at that particular time. And since then I had
made up my mind that I was going to tell him—you
know I had.'

'Yes, well.' Her mother gave a little shrug. 'So now
he knows. I think it was unfortunate to say the least
that he should have heard it from someone else, but
there it is, it's done now.' She paused and looked
searchingly at Ellie. 'But where do you go from
here?'

'Mum, I don't know!' Ellie shook her head.

'He'll want to see Jamie,' Barbara observed. 'It
stands to reason he will.'

'Then we'll just have to work something out, won't
we?' Ellie ran her fingers through her hair, the gesture
conveying more than a hint of the turmoil she was
experiencing. 'That was one of the reasons I didn't
want him to know. I can't see a lot of toing and froing
can be any good for Jamie.'

'He'll probably thank you for it when he's older,'
said Barbara. 'Every child needs to know its father.'

'Yes, well, maybe.' Ellie shrugged.

They were silent for a long moment then tentatively Barbara broached a question. 'Ellie,' she said slowly, 'you don't think there's any chance that you and Luke…?'

'Well, what do you think?' Ellie gave a short, dismissive laugh.

'I don't know, darling, I'm asking you,' Barbara replied mildly.

'The mood Luke's in at the moment, I wouldn't think there's a cat's chance,' Ellie replied.

'It would solve everything—for all of you.' Barbara stood up and carried the china and cutlery she had used to the dishwasher.

'Well, it isn't going to happen,' said Ellie tersely, 'so there's no point in even thinking about it.'

She may have told her mother not to even contemplate the possibility of herself and Luke getting together again, but for Ellie herself, when she was alone, it was a different matter. She knew that seeing Jamie and learning that the little boy was his had had a profound effect on Luke, more even than she'd thought it might, and it certainly raised the possibility that once he'd got over his shock and anger, he might want to try and make a go of things again purely for Jamie's sake. If that proved to be the case, Ellie really didn't know how she would feel about it. She knew she still had feelings for Luke, doubted they'd ever really gone away. That had been evident on several occasions since they had met up again, not least during their hostage situation, which had made her face up to what was important in her life and what wasn't. And Luke most definitely had been high on that important list. But how he felt about her was another matter altogether.

In the past he had most definitely not wanted commitment. Now he knew he had a son it might be different—but was that what she wanted? Deep down, she knew it wasn't—she wanted Luke to want her for herself, not because he felt he had to face up to his responsibilities.

It had been a shock—there was no denying that. Even after he'd suspected that Ellie's child might be his, it had still come as a shock when he'd actually seen the little boy and Ellie had confirmed the fact. Just for one moment he had felt a sense of wild elation, followed by puzzlement when he had tried to understand why Ellie hadn't told him. Puzzlement had quickly been replaced by a growing sense of anger that in all that time he had been in the States he had been a father and hadn't known a thing about it.

His child, Jamie, had been growing from a baby to a toddler then to a little boy and he'd missed out on everything. And not only that. He'd missed Ellie's pregnancy, the growing sense of anticipation and excitement and the birth itself. He would most definitely have been present at that—if only he'd known.

Seeing that little boy today, watching him run around, playing with him—it had done something to him, had touched something vital deep inside him, something he'd never before been aware of.

He spent the rest of that day prowling around his apartment, trying to get his head around everything and at times failing miserably as his anger and sense of frustration at all he had missed threatened to get the better of him.

It was early evening when his doorbell rang and he opened the door to find Reece Davies on the step with a six-pack of beer under one arm. 'Thought you could use some company, old man,' he said cheerfully.

'You know something, Reece…' Luke stepped aside to enable the older man to enter his flat '…you could well be right.'

'And I dare say you'll be watching the rugby,' Reece added as he collapsed in an armchair.

Luke hadn't even thought about watching the rugby on the television, but in a strange sort of way, sitting there with Reece, sipping cold beer and watching Wales play had a relaxing effect on him, and for a short space of time he forgot everything else.

It was only when the match was over and Reece, flushed and in a state of euphoria over a win for Wales, turned to him. 'So have you got over all your heroics?' he said.

'My heroics?' Luke frowned into his glass as the memories began creeping back.

'No point being modest, man, you're being hailed as a hero in the town.'

'I can't think why,' Luke muttered. 'I was as scared as the rest of them at the time.'

'Even so—stories of tourniquets and gunshot wounds are doing the rounds, not to mention the birth of a baby.'

'That was down to Ellie…' His frown grew deeper.

'And how is the lovely Ellie?' Reece threw him a sidelong glance. 'Have you seen her since…?'

'I went to see her today. Yes,' Luke shrugged. 'She's OK.'

'Fancy her, don't you?' said Reece, as blunt as ever.

'What?' Luke tried to look irritated but feared he failed miserably.

'No good pretending.' Reece gave a guffaw. 'I know these things and I know you've been drooling over our little locum ever since she set foot in the place. I could even go so far as to say it was pretty convenient you and she being holed up together overnight...'

'I can assure you it was nothing like that...'

'OK.' Reece held up his hands then tossed Luke another can of beer. 'Only joking.' He paused as he opened his own can and began pouring the beer into his glass. 'But are you going to do anything about it—now you know she isn't married, I mean?'

'It's not that simple.' Luke shook his head, wondering just how much he should divulge to Reece.

'Because of her baby, you mean?'

'Yes.' Luke nodded. 'Because of that. And that baby, by the way, is three years old.'

'Really—as old as that?' Reece looked surprised. 'Well, at least you know it wasn't a recent relationship,' he said. When Luke didn't reply, he lifted one eyebrow. 'Don't you?' he added.

'The relationship was with me,' said Luke quietly at last.

Reece had been flicking around from channel to channel with the television's remote control, but at Luke's words he grew still then switched the TV off.

'What do you mean?' he said at last, turning to Luke.

'What I say.' Luke shrugged. 'The relationship that Ellie had four years ago was with me. It was before I went to the States. We were both working at the same hospital at the time.'

Reece was staring at him in apparent amazement. 'And the baby…?' he said at last.

'Mine,' said Luke tersely.

'Yours!' Reece's jaw dropped. 'But when I told you she had a baby, you were surprised. You had no idea.'

'That's right, I had no idea,' Luke said, outwardly calm. But a nerve throbbed furiously at the side of his jaw, giving away his inner tension.

'Hang on a minute.' Reece set his glass down on the floor beside his chair. 'Let me get this straight. You're telling me that when you went off to the States to work you had no idea that Ellie was expecting your child?'

'That's right. She tells me now that she only found out just before I went.'

'And she didn't let you know?' Reece looked frankly incredulous now.

Luke shook his head. 'Actually,' he said, and almost found himself coming to Ellie's defence, 'we had agreed to end our relationship before I went…'

'Even so…I would have thought…'

'We didn't part on very good terms. She caught me with someone else at some party. There was nothing in it but…' He shrugged awkwardly.

'I still think it strange that she wouldn't want to tell you about something as important as a baby,' mused Reece. 'Most women, in my experience, would have been hounding you for maintenance,' he added gloomily, almost as if he had first-hand knowledge of that particular situation. 'Did she never want that?'

'Apparently not.' Luke shook his head. 'She didn't even seem inclined to tell me when we met up again at the surgery.'

'Why do you think that might be?' mused Reece.

Luke was silent for a while then, casting a sidelong glance in Reece's direction, he said, 'She did say something about how I never wanted to commit myself, never wanted to settle down...'

'And did you?' Reece raised one eyebrow.

'Not at one time I didn't, no...' he admitted grudgingly.

'What about when you were first seeing Ellie?'

'No, probably not then,' he said. He shrugged again. 'But neither did she. She also was very career-minded at that time.'

'We're not talking about Ellie, we're talking about you,' Reece reminded him. 'So at the time you went to the States, Ellie believed you weren't in any way interested in settling down, and at the same time you were having it away with someone else. For God's sake, man, do you wonder at it that she didn't want to tell you about the baby? She obviously didn't see you as good father material.'

'I soon realised I was wrong,' muttered Luke. 'I missed Ellie almost from the start. And I wasn't having it away, as you put it—at least, not then I wasn't. There were others, damn it—of course there were, four years is a long time—but none of them remotely compared with Ellie.'

'So what are you saying? That after you went to the States you wished you'd let Ellie know how much she'd meant to you?'

'Something like that, yes,' muttered Luke. Suddenly he was unable to meet Reece's gaze.

'OK, so what have you done about it?' Reece settled himself further back in the armchair and crossed his legs.

'I tried to talk to her,' said Luke, 'we had lunch together—just before the bank raid actually.'

'And did you get anywhere?'

'No, not really, but even before that...well, the main reason I came to this area to work was because I knew it was near Ellie's family home and I hoped we would meet up again.'

There was a long pause then Luke carried on speaking. 'I couldn't believe it when I heard she was coming to the practice as a locum.'

'I dare say it was a bit of a shock for her to find you there as well,' observed Reece dryly.

'Yes, I guess...' Luke nodded miserably. Looking across at Reece, he said, 'Do you know something? When we were in that hellhole, do you know what my biggest fear was?'

'No, go on.'

'That something would happen to Ellie. Right from the first when the gang burst in and it all started to go wrong and the first shot was fired, I was terrified that something might happen to her.'

'There were reports that they were holding you all as hostages and demanding a free passage out of there.' Reece's eyes narrowed. 'Is that true?'

'Yes.' Luke took a deep breath, knowing now that it wouldn't really matter if he spoke about the ordeal—at least, not to someone like Reece, a fellow doctor. 'I don't know how far it would have gone,' he went on as Reece listened intently. 'Luckily we managed to barricade ourselves inside the storeroom, but if they had managed to get at us again, I think they would have carried out their threats. They were very desperate men with little to lose. I think if they hadn't been given the transport they'd asked for they might have started picking us off one by one, and if they had been given it they would have taken one or perhaps two of us with them…then, who knows what would have happened? God knows what I would have done if they'd taken Ellie…' He trailed off then looked up sharply. 'We were separated at one point before we'd managed to barricade ourselves in. They marched me off to tend to one of their blokes who'd been shot and all the time I was doing that I was in agony that something might be happening to Ellie.'

Reece was silent for a long moment then with a level look at Luke he said, 'Do you know what I think, old man?' Not waiting for Luke to answer, he carried straight on. 'I don't think it should be me you're telling all this to, I think it should be Ellie.'

Luke passed his hands over his head, the gesture that summed up his frustration and helplessness. 'But will she want to hear it? She obviously doesn't think I'm good father material for her son. Maybe she wouldn't want to know how I feel about her.'

'Well…' Reece hauled himself to his feet then stood for a moment looking down at Luke. 'Maybe she would, maybe she wouldn't,' he said philosophically, 'but I guess there's only one way to find out.'

In the end Ellie was glad to go back to work, even if she was apprehensive at seeing Luke again. She knew they would have to talk, especially about Jamie and his future, and the thought filled her with trepidation. But she'd had her fill of moping around the house and, with her mother at work and Jamie back at nursery, there really wasn't anything for her to do. Neither did she feel she wanted to sit alone and dwell on the events of the past few days for any longer.

She was totally unprepared, however, for the huge welcome she received from her colleagues. There was no hint of what was to come when she encountered Luke in Reception. They were both early and the practice hadn't yet opened its doors for the day.

'Hello, Luke,' she said, wary of him, mindful of his anger of the previous day but nevertheless steadily meeting his gaze. There was no anger there in those tawny eyes this morning. Emotion certainly, although Ellie was hard-pushed to define that particular emotion, but not anger. He looked tired and the strain of all that had happened seemed to be etched in fine lines around his eyes. He appeared vulnerable and Ellie felt her heart go out to him.

'Hello, Ellie,' he said softly. 'I didn't know whether you would be in this morning or not.'

'I know it's Friday and the end of the week, but I couldn't see any point in staying away any longer,' she replied. 'I phoned William last night and I said I would be in.'

'Me, too,' Luke replied. He glanced around Reception as he spoke. 'It's very quiet,' he added. 'I wonder where everyone is?'

Ellie glanced at her watch. 'There's another twenty minutes before we open,' she said.

'Even so.' He shrugged. 'The girls are usually here, sorting the post and the notes for the day's surgeries. Are you going upstairs?' he asked, and when she nodded he fell into step beside her and they began to climb the wide staircase together. They were silent for most of the way then as they neared the top they both spoke together.

'Luke…' said Ellie.

'I was thinking…' said Luke. 'After you,' he went on with a short laugh.

'No, you go first,' she said. Anything to delay saying what needed to be said.

He took a deep breath. 'I was simply going to say that we need to talk,' he said.

'Yes,' she agreed as they reached the top of the stairs and turned into the long corridor, 'we do. We'll arrange a time and a place and we'll talk.'

'Right,' he said, then hesitated. 'What were you going to say?'

'I was going to say the same,' she said, stepping back as Luke opened the staffroom door.

'Good—' he began, then stopped, his words dramatically halted as they entered the room and were greeted by the sound of applause and cries of 'Welcome back!' from what appeared to be the entire staff of the practice.

Ellie gasped then froze on the spot, the colour draining from her face as she suffered a flashback to that dreadful moment in the bank when the gang had burst in and shrieked at everyone to fall to the floor. Luke either guessed what had happened to her or experienced the same reaction himself for he slipped his arm reassuringly around her before leading her forward.

William made a brief speech, officially welcoming Luke and Ellie back to work, saying how relieved they all were that they were safe, and how proud they all felt of them for their bravery. A glass each of champagne followed for everyone, then it was business as usual, with the receptionists, giggling slightly at the unexpectedness of the celebration, returning to open the doors to the public, the admin staff going to their offices and the doctors to their consulting rooms.

As Ellie had predicted, Oakminster was still agog over the drama that had been played out in its town centre, and every patient she saw that morning had something to say on the matter. Most pronounced their heartfelt relief that she and Dr Barron were safe, some had theories of their own as to how the police should have handled the situation while others were intensely curious as to how they had coped under such conditions.

'I can't imagine how you delivered that baby,' said one woman.

'Babies have a habit of coming when they are ready,' said Ellie.

'Yes, but even so,' the woman added darkly.

Another asked about Violet. 'Is it true she fought one of the robbers for her mobile phone?'

'Well, not quite.' Ellie suppressed a smile. 'Although, come to think of it, I'm sure she would have done if she'd had to.'

Towards the end of the morning she was asked if she would see an extra patient, and when she agreed she was surprised when Aileen walked into her room.

'Aileen!' she exclaimed, rising to her feet, 'I didn't expect to see you today!' In a purely spontaneous movement the two of them embraced like two long-lost friends.

'I didn't think you would be at work,' said Aileen.

'I got bored at home,' said Ellie with a little shrug. 'And it's been a difficult week here at the centre…'

'It's been a difficult week all round,' said Aileen grimly as she lowered herself into a chair.

'Are you having problems?' asked Ellie sympathetically.

'Yes, I am,' Aileen admitted, 'and I have to say I'm glad it is you I'm seeing. I couldn't imagine explaining it all to one of the other doctors—apart from Dr Barron, that is, and I'm not sure if he's back at work yet.'

'Yes, he is actually.' Ellie nodded. 'But tell me, what's troubling you?'

'Well, for a start I can't sleep,' said Aileen. 'I thought I would, I was so tired, but when it came to it that first night I just couldn't get off, and then last night it was the same. I just keep going over and over what happened in my head. I feel terrible as well. I keep thinking, what if...what if we hadn't been able to barricade ourselves in, what if they'd broken the door down... Honestly, it's stupid, I know...but...'

'It's not stupid at all,' Ellie replied. 'It's a perfectly normal reaction to coping with such a period of intense stress. Now, tell me, did you have any counselling at the hospital?'

'No.' Aileen shook her head. 'I didn't think I needed it. All I felt then was an overwhelming sense of relief that everything was all right. It's only been since that I've felt bad.'

'I'm going to arrange for you to have some counselling straight away,' said Ellie briskly, 'and I'm going to give you a light sedative to help you to sleep.'

'I don't want to become addicted to sleeping pills,' said Aileen dubiously.

'You won't,' Ellie replied. 'These will simply restore your sleep pattern.' She printed out the prescription and handed it to Aileen. 'I'll organise emergency counselling and you should get a call later today.'

'Thanks, Ellie.' Aileen stood up then looked down at Ellie. 'I don't think we'll ever forget what happened, do you?'

'Probably not,' Ellie agreed, 'but the images and memories will fade in time.'

'I hope so.' Aileen gave a little shudder. 'I spoke to Pauline this morning,' she added, as she turned to leave the room.

'Is she all right?' asked Ellie.

'Yes, she seems to be,' Aileen replied.

'And what about her son. Has she heard anything?'

'Yes, apparently he's turned up in an Indonesian hospital, suffering from malaria, but at least he's alive.'

'She must be very relieved.'

'She was on a bit of a high,' Aileen said. 'She also told me that Denise and baby Sam have gone home from hospital. Apparently the whole street turned out to welcome them home.'

'That's lovely.' Ellie smiled.

After Aileen had gone, a message came through from the hospital to say that surgery on Brian Westwood had been successful, and that the member of the gang who had been injured was recovering slowly.

And then, at the end of the morning, Luke appeared in the doorway of her consulting room. 'I see you've survived,' he said with a rueful grin. 'My morning has been nearly as eventful as the raid itself.'

'Mine, too,' Ellie said. 'Everyone seemed to have a take on it or even simply wanted to tell me where they were and what they were doing when they heard the news.'

'It's going to take Oakminster some time to forget

this,' said Luke. 'That is, if they ever do. I guess it will go down in history as the summer of the bank raid.' He paused and looked searchingly at her. 'Are you OK?' he said.

'Yes, I think so…' She brushed a stray wisp of hair away from her face, tucking it behind her ear.

'I wondered earlier…when we arrived… It was a bit overwhelming, wasn't it?'

'Yes,' she agreed, 'it was. I'm afraid I suffered a flashback. I suppose it was the suddenness of it but it took me right back to that awful moment when they burst through the doors of the bank…' Her voice faltered slightly.

'I know,' said Luke. 'I know exactly what you mean. But we can't blame them, they thought they were doing the right thing.'

'Oh, I know,' said Ellie quickly. 'I'm not blaming them—they don't know, do they?'

'No.' Luke shook his head. 'Like with most things, you never fully understand a situation unless you've experienced it at first hand. None of them could possibly know what it means to accept the fact that you might be facing a violent death.'

'No,' whispered Ellie, shaking her head. 'But we do, don't we?' Helpless tears sprang to her eyes as she stared up at Luke.

'Yes,' he said softly. Reaching across her desk, he smoothed her tears away as they began to trickle down her cheeks. 'Yes, we know exactly.'

'Somehow it makes everything look different.'

'Yes,' he agreed, his own voice suddenly husky, 'yes, it does.' He hesitated for a moment then he said, 'I would have asked you to have lunch with me, but that might not be a good idea under the circumstances, in spite of the fact that I know a nice little place that serves the most delicious hot cheese scones.'

Ellie smiled and brushed away a final stray tear.

'Instead,' Luke went on, not giving her the chance to comment, 'I wonder if dinner might be more appropriate? How about I pick you up from home at seven-thirty?'

'I think,' said Ellie, taking a deep breath. 'That sounds like a very good idea.'

CHAPTER TWELVE

'MUM, would you look after Jamie for me this evening, please?'

'Is this what I think it might be?' Barbara looked at Ellie over the top of her glasses.

'It is.' Ellie gave a faint smile. 'Luke has asked me to have dinner with him.'

'Ah,' said Barbara, and there was a decided note of satisfaction in the one syllable.

'Don't go reading anything into it,' Ellie warned. 'There is a tremendous amount to sort out.'

'OK.' Barbara shrugged. 'But I'll be living in hope.'

'Mum, you're impossible,' said Ellie with a laugh.

'Maybe, but I don't see why some situations shouldn't have a happy ending. Where is he taking you?'

'The Italian restaurant in Oakminster,' Ellie replied. 'He's picking me up at seven-thirty.'

She agonised over what she should wear, in the end settling for a pair of black trousers in a soft, floaty material and a top with thin shoulder straps that was neither green nor grey but a shade somewhere between the two, a sort of ethereal sea-green, a shade she knew suited her colouring and complexion. Her hair she caught up in a jewelled clasp, allowing soft tendrils to frame her face, and if she had still been in any doubt over her appearance, the look in Luke's eyes when he stopped outside the cottage at seven and she walked to his car told her all she needed to know.

'You look lovely, Ellie,' he said, confirming the fact as she slid into the passenger seat beside him.

She knew her mother was at the window of the cottage, watching them, and as they drew away she lifted her hand in farewell.

'Your mum?' said Luke, seeing the gesture.

'Yes.' With a little sigh Ellie settled down in the soft leather seat.

'And Jamie?' he said quietly.

'He's asleep,' she replied.

'Ah,' he said, and she could have sworn she detected a note of tenderness in his voice. She threw him a sidelong glance, but his profile was set, giving away nothing further of his thoughts. He looked impossibly handsome tonight in a light-coloured linen jacket and trousers and a deep red, open-necked shirt.

They were silent for a time as he drove towards Oakminster then he spoke again. 'I want to know all about him, Ellie,' he said.

'Yes, of course.' She felt a stab of something she couldn't quite define. Was it only Jamie he was interested in? She knew he would want to know things, that was inevitable. But were her worst fears about to be realised in that his only interest would be in their child and not in her? She had seen the look in his eyes when he had greeted her, but did that really prove anything or was it simply the appreciation any man might show towards his date for the evening when she had made the effort to look her best?

They parked the car then strolled to the restaurant, which was tucked away in a tiny side street. Since the thunderstorm the fierce heat of the summer had subsided, giving way to clearer, fresher weather, but the evening was still warm and balmy with a high mackerel sky, while swallows swooped and dived high above them in their quest for food.

In the restaurant they were shown to a table at the rear of the building beside French doors that opened onto the gardens where a small waterfall tumbled over rocks and into a pool of pebbles, and where statues of Roman gods were set amongst the backdrop of dark green shrubbery, subtly lit by concealed lighting.

When they were settled with drinks, after ordering their meal, Luke leaned back in his chair and observed her shrewdly. 'So tell me about him,' he said simply at last.

'What do you want to know?'

'Everything,' he replied.

Ellie took a deep breath and for the next hour she talked solely about Jamie. She told about his birth, the date he was born, his birth weight, the colour of his eyes and his hair.

'Was anyone with you?' he wanted to know. 'At the birth, I mean?'

'Yes,' she replied, 'my mother.' And her answer seemed to satisfy him.

'I owe her a lot,' she said. 'She's been there for me through everything,' she went on. 'She helped me when I was pregnant, when Jamie was born, when he was a baby…and ever since really. Actually, I don't know what I would have done without her.'

'When did you move in with her?' he asked.

'Just before the birth.' Ellie stared down into her glass, remembering how it had been at that time. 'I hadn't intended to stay,' she went on after a moment, 'but somehow…I don't know, it seemed the simplest solution all round. Mum was finding the cottage a bit large on her own so I hope I've been able to help her in that respect.'

Their antipasti arrived and she told him about Jamie starting at nursery and of how she'd eventually gone back to work. 'Locum work suited me fine,' she explained. 'It wasn't too demanding and I found I could usually just work part time, which left me plenty of time to be with Jamie.'

Throughout their main course she talked about those little things in the development of any child, which were probably only important to those closest to the child—when he cut his first tooth, his first steps, his favourite toys and the first words he'd spoken. 'He likes trains,' she said, 'and kicking a ball— but you already know that.'

'What doesn't he like?' asked Luke.

'Let me see.' Ellie reflected for a moment. 'Well, he doesn't like cockerels,' she said at last.

'Cockerels?' Luke raised his eyebrows in surprise.

'Yes, cockerels.' Ellie nodded then went on to explain, 'But that was because one crowed quite close to his buggy when he was little more than a baby. It frightened him and he hasn't liked them ever since. But that's about all really—he's a very happy little boy. He adores a blue, cuddly elephant that my mum bought him, he takes it everywhere with him and refuses to sleep at night unless he has it.'

'I've missed so much,' said Luke sadly, shaking his head. 'I have so much time to make up—that is, if you'll let me, Ellie?'

'Of course,' she said. 'We'll have to work something out so that you can build up a relationship with Jamie.'

'Yes,' he agreed, then after a moment's silence said, 'But where does that leave you and me?'

Her heart leapt at his words but she couldn't be sure of their meaning. 'I don't know,' she said, shaking her head. 'Where do you want it to be?'

'It's more what you want,' he said.

'Not entirely,' she said quickly. 'You were the one who couldn't ever contemplate the idea of any sort of commitment or long-term relationship.'

'Maybe that was true of me once,' he agreed ruefully, 'but that was a long time ago, Ellie. Maybe I've changed now.'

'So what are you saying?' She stared at him, her fork poised halfway to her mouth.

'That maybe we could try again—a fresh start, so to speak?'

Her pulse quickened at his words but they still did nothing to allay her fears that it would only be for Jamie that he was prepared to give their relationship another try. She lowered the fork to her plate, the food uneaten. On the other hand, would that be such a bad thing? No doubt in time Jamie would be delighted that his parents had made the effort to make a go of things and maybe, just maybe, in doing so, they might re-create the magic they had once shared.

'Ellie?' Luke lowered his head in order to be able to look into her face, obviously waiting for her answer.

She pushed her plate away then cleared her throat. 'Yes,' she said at last, 'we could certainly try—I don't know whether or not it will work,' she added quickly when she saw a light come into his eyes. 'It's been a long time…'

'I know,' he agreed, 'but I feel we owe it to Jamie to at least give it a try.'

She nodded, her heart sinking again at his words. There it was again, the implication that it would only be for Jamie.

'I think,' she managed to say at last, and her voice sounded strange even to herself, not like her voice at all, 'that if we are to do this we need to take things very slowly, very slowly indeed.'

'Of course.' His eyes widened innocently, as if it was inconceivable that he should have even contemplated anything else.

'I would need to introduce you into Jamie's world very gradually, giving him ample time to get to know you. You have to remember that he isn't used to having a man around.'

'Perhaps we could start by taking him out together...'

'Where do you mean?' She sounded dubious.

'Well, to a children's playground or something like that. Isn't that what children like—swings and slides and things?'

'Yes, of course...'

'Well, then, it would be a start.' He paused while the waiter cleared their plates then, after he'd ordered coffee for them both, he glanced around the restaurant and said, 'We need to do this sort of thing again as well—just you and me, Ellie.'

'Yes,' she agreed, 'but, like I say, we can't just rush in and carry on where we left off. We need to take things very slowly.'

'Absolutely,' he said firmly, his expression implacable.

They lingered over coffee, lulled by the sound of

soft background music and the ripple of water running over the pebbles in the garden, then casually Luke asked Ellie if she'd suffered any further flashbacks that day.

'No.' She shook her head. 'I think it was just the shock of our unexpected welcome back to the surgery that did it—I've been all right since.'

'It may well happen again,' he said. 'Shock is a strange thing and can have long-term effects.'

'Yes, I know,' she agreed. 'The thing is, I suppose you just can't imagine that anything like that will ever happen to you. I guess we were fortunate that we all escaped with our lives.' She paused reflectively, then added, 'Goodness knows how the survivors cope after some of the appalling terrorist attacks we hear about.'

'Do you know what the worst part was for me?' he said after a moment.

'No.' She shook her head.

'When you and I were separated. I was terrified that something would happen to you...' As he spoke he stretched out his hand across the table and covered hers.

She looked up sharply, her heart leaping at his touch. 'Oh, Luke,' she said, her voice choked, almost a whisper. 'It was the same for me too,' she admitted. 'When they took you off I nearly went to pieces. It was only the fact that the others needed me—looked to me because I was a doctor—that kept me going. I had to help them, do my best for them, but all the while I couldn't stop thinking about you, agonising about what was happening, where they had taken you and what they wanted you for...' She trailed off, unable to continue.

'Ellie...' His hand tightened over hers.

'When you came back into that room,' she went on at last, 'well, I've never been so relieved in all my life—it was almost as if it didn't matter what happened after that because I knew you were safe.'

'I felt the same.' His voice was thick with emotion. After a long moment of silence, during which they simply stared helplessly at each other, he beckoned the waiter to their table. 'I think we'll go,' he said.

They left the restaurant in silence then strolled back to the car. Luke's arm was around Ellie's shoulders and when they reached the car and stopped, Luke turned and drew her into his arms. As Ellie lifted her face for his kiss and his mouth covered hers, it felt as if at long last she'd finally come home.

Luke stretched. Putting his hands behind his head, he linked his fingers and relaxed. He still couldn't quite believe what had happened. One minute he and Ellie had been in the restaurant after spending a pleasant evening enjoying a meal and talking about Jamie and the next, well! If anyone had told him what would happen he really wouldn't have believed them. Especially after he and Ellie had both agreed that if they were to try and rebuild their relationship in any way, it would have to be done very, very slowly.

Already he had imagined a long, slow process of dates, flowers, chocolates and all those other things that a woman wanted in order to be convinced that a man loved her, not to mention endless talking about why their relationship had ended and what they could do to prevent the same thing happening again. There was a part of him that dreaded all that. He didn't mind the chocolates and flowers routine so much but he wasn't good at talking about his feelings and even worse at analysing why he had acted in a certain way—but he was quite resigned to all of it if that was what it was going to take to get Ellie back into his life again.

That was why what had happened next had come as such a surprise, albeit a delightful one. He couldn't quite remember how it had happened. He remembered leaving the restaurant and walking back to the car, he remembered slipping his arm around Ellie, wondering if she would shrug it away but at the same time somehow feeling confident that she wouldn't. Why had he felt that sudden confidence? He frowned, trying hard to recall, then it came to him. It had been because Ellie had admitted that during the raid the worst part for her had been when she'd thought something had happened to him and the best part had been when he'd walked back into the room and she'd known he was safe. Surely that proved that she still felt something for him? Well, whatever, it had given him the confidence not only to put his arm around her but when they had got back to the car to draw her into his arms and kiss her.

It was what had happened next that was still a bit of a blur in his mind. She had responded to his kiss— that much he had hoped for—but what he hadn't quite bargained for was the measure of that response. It had started sedately enough but passion had flared between them like a flame that had been merely flickering, starved of oxygen, and had suddenly been revived. And then the passion had exploded and somehow, by an unspoken agreement, they had found themselves here in his apartment and, incredibly, it was as if they'd never been apart.

Turning his head gently, so as not to disturb her,

he looked down at Ellie where she lay beside him in his bed. Her eyes were closed, her hair spread out across the pillow, her lashes sweeping the soft curve of her cheek. A sheet covered her nakedness, gently moulding itself over the rounded contours of her body, and as he watched her, Luke's heart suffused with love.

Their love-making had been every bit as good as it had ever been, causing him to agonise afresh how he could ever have let her go.

Even as he watched her, she opened her eyes. 'You were watching me,' she said, but there was no trace of accusation in her voice. 'What were you thinking?'

'I was wondering what happened to our agreement to take things very slowly,' he said with a deep chuckle.

A smile touched her lips. 'It wasn't quite according to plan,' she agreed wryly.

'Are you complaining?' Taking one hand from behind his head, he gently traced a line down the side of her face with his finger.

'How could I complain about that?' she said.

'We are good together, Ellie,' he said. 'We always were, which makes me realise even more that we should never have parted.'

'You regret us parting?' she said softly, reaching up her own hand and touching his face.

'How can you ask that?' He gave a deep sigh. 'Of course I regret it.'

'Because of Jamie, you mean?' she said, and somehow she seemed to be holding her breath as she waited for his reply.

'No.' He shook his head. 'Not just because of Jamie. I mean because of us. I deeply regret the fact that we've lost four years of our lives, four years that we could have spent together.'

'You weren't ready to settle down, Luke,' she reminded him.

'Maybe I thought I wasn't at the time,' he said, 'but I soon found out I was wrong, believe me.'

'What do you mean?' She moved slightly in order to be able to look into his face and the sheet slipped, revealing the curve of her breast.

'I missed you from the very start,' he said quietly. There, he'd admitted it now. 'I knew almost as soon as I reached the States that I'd made a huge mistake.'

'But…your career…?'

'Oh, career-wise it was good, but personally it simply wasn't right. Well, at that point I really didn't think there was any going back. Where you were concerned I really thought I'd blown it, especially after that episode at the club with…Sarah…'

'Don't you mean Susie?' She raised one eyebrow.

'Was that her name? I don't know, Sarah, Susie, it makes no difference because it really wasn't important. Anyway, I thought you wouldn't want to know, especially after I wrote to you and you didn't reply.'

'I didn't know you'd written.' She frowned. 'Where did you send the letter?'

'To the hospital, asking them to forward it if you'd moved on, but if you didn't receive it maybe they didn't.'

'That must have been after I'd left and moved in with Mum,' she said slowly, wondering how she would have reacted at the time if she had received his letter.

'Well, whatever.' He shrugged. 'But when I didn't hear from you I imagined you really didn't want to know so I decided the only thing I could do was to get on with my life and put the past behind me.'

'And did you?' asked Ellie tentatively.

'To a point,' he said. 'But the thing was, you wouldn't go away, Ellie.'

'What do you mean, I wouldn't go away?' She frowned.

'Exactly what I say.' Gently he began smoothing her hair away from her face. 'You were always there at the edges of my mind. I was always thinking about you, wondering what you were doing, whether or not you were with anyone else or if you ever thought about me. I...I couldn't bear the thought of you with someone else, Ellie...that was why I found it so unbearable when I came back and found that you had a baby... I thought you had someone else...'

'So why did you come back,' she said, 'and why Oakminster?'

'I wanted to find you,' he said, 'and when I saw the advertisement for a doctor in Oakminster I thought that would be a good place to start as it was so close to your family home. I knew it was only a slim chance, that you had probably moved away years ago, but I reckoned I had to start somewhere. I'd already phoned the hospital and they said you'd left shortly after I had and that they had no forwarding address for you.'

'So are you saying that you came to Oakminster deliberately?' Ellie's eyes widened.

'Well, yes,' he admitted. 'I thought it might be a way of making contact with you again. I have to say, though, that I simply couldn't believe it when you applied for the post of locum.'

'Luke...'

'Yes?'

'Come here.' To his delight Ellie reached up and wound her arms around his neck, her intentions more than obvious. Stretching out above her, he took her face between his hands, his fingers tangled in her hair, and as his lips met hers, for the second time that evening he felt the familiar stirring of desire.

It was late when he finally took her home, very late, but Barbara was still awake and she called out softly as Ellie tiptoed up the stairs.

'Ellie,' she said, 'are you all right?'

Gently Ellie pushed open her mother's bedroom door and stood there in the doorway. 'Sorry it's so late,' she said. 'I thought you would be asleep. Was Jamie all right?'

'Jamie was fine,' Barbara replied from her bed. 'What about you?'

'Oh, yes,' Ellie replied, 'I'm fine, too.'

'Well, I'm glad to hear it. Your evening was obviously a success.'

'Yes, Mum, it was—a great success. I'll tell you about it in the morning.'

'All right. Goodnight, darling.'

''Night, Mum.' She backed out of the room and pulled the door to behind her, then she walked softly across the landing to Jamie's room. The little boy was fast asleep, his head burrowed into his pillow, face turned to the side, his bottom in the air and his toy elephant beside him. She stood for a long moment just looking down at him, and in the light from his bedside nightlight she could quite clearly see the little boy's resemblance to his father—the shape of his head and the outline of his profile against the whiteness of the pillow—and her heart ached with a sudden surge of love for him.

She still couldn't quite believe what had happened that night. She had surprised herself when she had found herself telling Luke how frightened she had been for his safety during the raid, and then it had given her something of a warm glow when he had admitted he had felt the same thing about her. She had felt comfortable with their agreement to give their relationship another try and although she had been the one to insist that they take things very slowly and Luke had agreed, it seemed events had spiralled right out of her control when they had left the restaurant.

From the moment he had taken her in his arms all the old feelings and sensations had come flooding back and it was as if they'd never been apart. His kiss had stirred half-forgotten memories, releasing desire so powerful that it had threatened to overwhelm them both. Somehow they had found themselves in his apartment, where in their haste to possess each other once again their clothes had formed a trail into the bedroom. And then…then had come that wonderful, glorious, bitter-sweet moment when they had become one and all the pent-up frustrations and unrequited passion of the past few years had finally been satisfied.

And as if all that hadn't been enough, later, when they had lain in the glorious aftermath of their love-making there had come that incredible moment when Luke had admitted that he had made a mistake in leaving her, that he had missed her from the very start and that his sole reason for returning had been to find her again, even going to the lengths of taking a job in the same area where he knew she had once lived.

It had doubtless been a shock to him to learn of Jamie's existence, but where she had feared he would remain angry with her for not telling him, it now seemed he was acknowledging his share of the blame in as much as he shouldn't have left in the way he had.

At that moment Jamie moved, wriggling onto his back and flinging one arm out sideways and the other across his forehead. Ellie leaned over the bed and softly kissed his cheek, at the same time pulling the cover over him. Jamie, of course, couldn't know, but Ellie knew that from that day forward their lives were about to change beyond all recognition.

'So what happens next?' Barbara poured her daughter a second mug of tea and passed it across the table. It was early the following morning and she'd just heard a somewhat edited version of the events of the previous evening.

'He's coming round after breakfast,' Ellie replied. 'I thought perhaps we'd take Jamie for a walk.'

'You know, darling, I'm so happy for you.' Suddenly there were tears in Barbara's eyes.

'Thanks, Mum.'

'What made you both realise in the end?'

'I'm not really sure.' Ellie frowned. 'Several things, I think. What happened during the bank raid and realising that death could have been just a moment away and…and Jamie, of course.'

'But not just Jamie?'

'No, not just Jamie.' Ellie shook her head. 'Luke told me he knew he'd made a mistake as soon as he got to the States, that he'd missed me from the start. And do you know? He said he came back here and got a job in Oakminster purely in the hope that he would see me again…'

'Well, you can't doubt that, Ellie, can you?'

'No. I don't think I can.' She paused. 'But, Mum, I've been thinking, what about you—if Luke and I— well, what would you do? You've already said that this place is too much for you on your own…' She trailed off uncertainly.

'I would sell,' Barbara replied firmly. 'I had half decided to do that before you came here, so that is what I would do. It's time I had something much smaller—a little flat or something.'

'But you love this cottage. Dad…' Ellie shook her head, unable to continue.

'Your father would have been the last person to want me to carry on here if it was too much for me,' said Barbara firmly. 'But if you feel that badly about the place, maybe when I've found my little flat, you and Luke should come and live here.'

Ellie stared at her.

'Don't look so shocked,' her mother said lightly. 'It could be a perfect solution all round, don't you think?'

'Well, yes,' said Ellie faintly, 'I suppose it could. But all this is moving too fast…'

'It might be worth mentioning to Luke, though, when the subject arises, as I'm sure it will.'

'Well, yes, maybe…'

Barbara lifted her head. 'Is that Jamie I can hear?'

'Yes, he must have just woken up. I'll go up and fetch him.'

'Yes, you had better,' Barbara replied crisply, 'es-pecially if we are expecting a visitor shortly.'

*   *   *

By the time Luke arrived Jamie was up and dressed and finishing his boiled egg and toast soldiers. Ellie went through into the hall, leaving Jamie with her mother. When she opened the front door Luke was standing on the step.

'Hello,' he said softly, his eyes meeting hers.

'Good morning,' she replied. 'I trust you slept well?'

'Not that well, actually.' Humour lurked deep in those tawny eyes. 'I found it incredibly difficult to get to sleep and when I did my dreams were so disturbing they kept waking me up.'

'They must be to do with all the incredible events in your life in the last few days,' Ellie replied as she stepped into his arms and wound her own arms around his neck.

'Absolutely,' he replied softly as his mouth claimed hers.

She gave herself up entirely to the luxury of his kiss and failed to notice that Jamie had left the kitchen and had come to stand beside them. When at last both she and Luke drew apart it was to find the little boy staring up at them in apparent awe.

Luke recovered first and, bending down so that his gaze was level with that of his son, he said, 'Hi, there, Jamie.'

'Hi,' Jamie replied solemnly, then with a frown he peered into Luke's face. 'Football,' he said at last in recognition.

'That's right,' said Luke with a laugh. 'You go and get your football, Jamie, and we'll go across to the green for a game.' As the little boy ran off into the garden, Luke stood up.

'He remembered you,' said Ellie softly.

'Yes,' Luke agreed, 'he did. I'm glad about that, seeing I'm going to be around from now on.' He turned then paused as he would have taken Ellie in his arms once more. 'Tell me something,' he said. 'When I was away, did you miss me at all?'

'Did I miss you?' Ellie wrinkled her nose, considering. 'Now, let me see…'

'Maybe just a little bit?' he said hopefully.

'Luke,' she said, looking up into his face and growing serious as his arms went around her again, 'I didn't just miss you a little bit, I missed you every moment of every day. And after Jamie was born he was so like you that every time I looked at him it was as if you were still there beside me.'

'And now I am,' he said softly, his lips against her hair.

'Yes,' she agreed, 'now you are. And do you know something, Dr Barron? This time I'm never ever going to let you go.'

'I'm glad to hear it,' he murmured. In the moment before his mouth claimed hers again he added, 'Even though I've no intention of going anywhere without you ever again.'

1105/059/MB144

Introducing a very special holiday collection

Inside you'll find

Roses for Christmas *by Betty Neels*
Eleanor finds herself working with the forceful Fulk van
Hensum from her childhood – and sees that he hasn't
changed. So why does his engagement to another woman
upset her so much?

Once Burned *by Margaret Way*
Celine Langton ends her relationship with Guy Harcourt
thinking he deserves someone more sophisticated. But why
can't she give back his ring?

A Suitable Husband *by Jessica Steele*
When Jermaine begins working with Lukas Tavinor,
she realises he's the kind of man she's always dreamed of
marrying. Does it matter that her sister feels the same way?

On sale Friday 7th October 2005

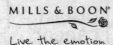

MILLS & BOON®

Live the emotion

Her Nine Month Miracle

She's having his baby!

In October 2005, By Request brings back
three favourite romances by bestselling
Mills & Boon authors:

The Pregnancy Discovery
by Barbara Hannay

The Baby Scandal
by Cathy Williams

Emergency Wedding
by Marion Lennox

Pick up these passionate stories.

On sale 7th October 2005

researching the cure

The facts you need to know:

- **One woman in nine** in the United Kingdom will develop breast cancer during her lifetime.

- Each year **40,700** women are newly diagnosed with breast cancer and around **12,800** women will die from the disease. However, survival rates are improving, with on average 77 per cent of women still alive five years later.

- **Men can also suffer from breast cancer**, although currently they make up less than one per cent of all new cases of the disease.

Britain has one of the highest breast cancer death rates in the world. Breast Cancer Campaign wants to understand why and do something about it. Statistics cannot begin to describe the impact that breast cancer has on the lives of those women who are affected by it and on their families and friends.

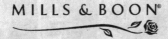

MILLS & BOON®

**During the month of October
Harlequin Mills & Boon will donate
10p from the sale of every
Modern Romance™ series book to
help Breast Cancer Campaign
in _researching the cure._**

Breast Cancer Campaign's scientific projects
look at improving diagnosis and treatment
of breast cancer, better understanding how
it develops and ultimately either curing the
disease or preventing it.

Do your part to help

Visit <u>www.breastcancercampaign.org</u>

And make a donation today.

researching the cure

Breast Cancer Campaign is a company limited by guarantee registered in England and
Wales. Company No. 05074725. Charity registration No. 299758.

4 Books
and a surprise gift!

We would like to take this opportunity to thank you for reading this Mills & Boon® book by offering you the chance to take FOUR more specially selected titles from the Medical Romance™ series absolutely FREE! We're also making this offer to introduce you to the benefits of the Reader Service™—

- ★ **FREE home delivery**
- ★ **FREE gifts and competitions**
- ★ **FREE monthly Newsletter**
- ★ **Exclusive Reader Service offers**
- ★ **Books available before they're in the shops**

Accepting these FREE books and gift places you under no obligation to buy, you may cancel at any time, even after receiving your free shipment. Simply complete your details below and return the entire page to the address below. You don't even need a stamp!

YES! Please send me 4 free Medical Romance books and a surprise gift. I understand that unless you hear from me, I will receive 6 superb new titles every month for just £2.75 each, postage and packing free. I am under no obligation to purchase any books and may cancel my subscription at any time. The free books and gift will be mine to keep in any case.

M5ZEF

Ms/Mrs/Miss/Mr ....Initials..
BLOCK CAPITALS PLEASE

Surname ....

Address ....

....

....Postcode ....

Send this whole page to:
UK: FREEPOST CN81, Croydon, CR9 3WZ